The Arnolfini

ART *Mysteries*

Rich
DiSILVIO

Author's Website: www.richdisilvio.com

- - - - - - - - - - - - - - - - - -

Names: DiSilvio, Rich
Title: The Arnolfini Art Mysteries
Description: New York, USA: DV Books, an imprint of Digital Vista, inc.
Identifiers: ISBN 978-1-950052-02-8 (paperback) |
ISBN 978-1-950052-03-5 (eBook)
Subjects: Short Stories | Art Crimes | Mysteries, Thrillers |
Private Investigator | Artists, Composers
Illustrations/Photos: 31

THE AUTHOR

Rich DiSilvio is an author of thrillers, mysteries, historical fiction and nonfiction. He has written books, historical articles, and commentaries for magazines and online resources. His passion for history, art, music, and architecture has yielded contributions in each discipline in his professional careers.

DiSilvio's work in the entertainment industry includes projects for historical documentaries, including James Cameron's *The Lost Tomb of Jesus*, *Killing Hitler*, *The War Zone* series, *Return to Kirkuk*, *Operation Valkyrie*, and cable TV shows and films such as *Tracey Ullman's State of the Union*, *Celebrity Mole*, *Blood Ties*, *Monty Python: Almost the Truth*, and many others.

He has written commentaries on the great composers (such as the top-rated Franz Liszt Site), and conceived and designed the Pantheon of Composers porcelain collection for the Metropolitan Opera, which also retailed throughout the USA and Europe.

His artwork and new media projects have graced the album covers and animated advertisements for numerous super-groups and celebrities, including, Pink Floyd, Yes, The Moody Blues, Cher, Madonna, Jay-Z, Willie Nelson, Miles Davis, the Rolling Stones, Alice Cooper, Queen, and many more.

As a software designer/developer, Rich pioneered the first interactive CD-ROM for educating staff and parents about Applied Behavioral Analysis (ABA) for training individuals with autism.

Rich lives in New York with his wife and has four children.

Contents

THE PHANTOM FORGER

Bernard Higley gasped as a large flake of paint peeled off of Antonello da Messina's long-lost masterpiece, the *Messina Madonna*. He had merely wiped the canvas with a fine linen cloth to remove what appeared to be a smudge, but a small chunk of oil paint peeled away and fell to the floor. He moved closer, in shock, as his eyes widened.

Bernard had been enthralled to acquire the prized find, being that it was last recorded as being seen in 1608. As curator of the *Cloisters Museum* in upper Manhattan, Bernard Higley was making preparations for a huge promotional campaign to herald the historic find, along with presenting three other recent acquisitions dating from the Renaissance era. But the *Messina Madonna* was the focal point, and Bernard had intentions of premièring the work early next year, in February of 1979, the five-hundredth anniversary of Messina's death.

As Bernard stepped even closer, he could feel his heart erratically accelerating as beads of sweat formed along his receding hairline. "Dear Lord! This can't be!" he frantically whimpered. He turned and ran past the stacks of paintings and priceless artifacts in the museum's storage chamber to the phone, and placed a call to the only person he could entrust to help him, Armand Arnolfini.

Thirty minutes later, at 6:52 AM, Armand entered the medieval complex. The *Cloisters Museum* was an historic assemblage of five ancient French cloisters that had been dismantled and shipped to New York in the 1930s to be reconstructed, along with their exquisite gardens. The munificent gift was by John D. Rockefeller Jr., who had also purchased the scenic property across the Hudson River to ensure it stayed undeveloped, as not to destroy the *Cloisters'* bucolic ambience. Armand walked past a series of Gothic archways, ancient tapestries and wood-carved bas-reliefs, then descended to the lowest level.

Bernard ran to greet him, as he gushed, "Armand! I'm so happy you could make it, especially at this early hour and on such short notice. I do apologize, but this is a most urgent and distressing matter."

"I sensed that on the phone, Bernie," Armand said as he yawned and massaged his sleepy eyes.

Armand Arnolfini was six-foot-two with jet-black wavy hair, finely chiseled features, and a muscular body from his three years of playing professional fútbol when he lived in Italy eight years ago. "What's the problem?"

Bernard swallowed hard. "I recently purchased a Messina, the *Messina Madonna*. And—"

"*The* 'Messina Madonna!?'" Armand blurted, surprised, and now awake.

Armand was not a typical private detective, as he previously worked for the FBI heading their Art Crimes division, which unfortunately disbanded due to America's lack of interest in the field. And that his father had been the curator of the *Uffizi Gallery* for twenty-two years and a professor of art history for many years thereafter, Armand was an expert in his own right, so he knew well the history and significance of Messina's long-lost portrait.

Antonello da Messina might not have risen to the high echelon of fame as da Vinci or Michelangelo, but it was Messina, who, being twenty-two years older than Leonardo, introduced the art of oil painting in Italy, having learned the technique from the alleged inventor himself; the Flemish master Jan van Eyck. As such, Messina had played a pivotal role in enlightening and inspiring the budding crop of painters in Italy who would propel the Italian Renaissance to the apex of creativity.

Meanwhile, Bernard hesitated in his response, "Well, uh, yes, it's the one and only *Messina Madonna*, Armand. However—"

"That's fantastic, Bernie! You must be overjoyed to acqu—"

"Hold on!" Bernard interjected. "I must tell you what happened."

As Armand's elation turned quizzical, Bernard continued, "I was simply wiping a smudge off the canvas when a chunk of paint peeled off."

Armand's concern transformed into a smile. "You had me worried, Bernie. We both know plenty of restorers who can repair it."

Bernard grimaced. "Armand, yes, it can be repaired, but that would only hide its dishonorable sins. What has been revealed through the portal that chip presented is most disturbing."

Armand squinted. "Are you saying there's another painting underneath?"

"Yes, but it's not an earlier painting, Armand. That would have been a relief, as it could explain it being a previous work by Messina that the master decided was substandard, and thus painted over it."

Armand rubbed his chin. "So you're saying there is a newer work underneath. How can that be? Are you sure?"

"Come, see for yourself."

Bernard escorted Armand to the *Cloisters'* subterranean conservation and storage chamber, with its modern nineteen-seventies tiled floor, muted-white walls, and where the air temperature and humidity was precisely controlled. Walking past a string of artifacts and tapestries from the medieval to Renaissance eras, they arrived at the *Messina Madonna,* which was sitting on a large oak easel.

Armand's eyes widened as he took a double-step to inspect it closer. "Good God!" His head swung toward Bernard. "A newer work, indeed!" He turned back to the painting and its disturbing aperture that Bernard had enlarged, thus revealing a large fragment of the unwelcome image underneath. "It appears to be a portion of a crucifixion. And, yes, by a modern surrealist."

"Exactly, Armand. Not being well versed in modern art, I am at a loss as to whom this mysterious artist might be. But more importantly, whom this repugnant forger of Renaissance masters must be, who didn't even have the decency to use a blank canvas. It's just an added slap in the face."

Armand leaned forward and peered behind the painting. He scratched the back of the canvas and smelled it, then looked back at Bernard. "It even looks and smells old."

"Yes, the forger somehow did a fine job of making the canvas appear old all right. Enough to fool my staff and I."

Armand gazed back at the aperture, and at the bright-colored paint beneath the dark-varnished veneer of the faux Renaissance oils. Pensively, he paused for a moment, then said, "I wonder if it's possible that the painting underneath is a masterwork by Magritte or Dali. The style fits."

Bernard shook his throbbing head. "Why on earth would someone cover a new masterwork with a fake old one?"

"One never knows what is and isn't possible, Bernie. My father had told me that during World War Two some museum officials had several of their masterpieces painted over with works by unknown artists to prevent Nazi thieves from stealing their priceless assets."

"Then I could only hope that what lies beneath this Messina is a Magritte or Dali, Armand. Only then could I recoup my financial blunder. I spent two hundred and fifty thousand dollars for this piece."

Armand cringed. "Ouch!"

"Ouch, indeed," Bernard uttered dejectedly. "We anticipated a Messina revival. But now those hopes are dashed. However, Jim Matteson, my restorer, is on his way here now to strip it completely. Then we shall have a better idea of what we're dealing with."

Three hours later, Jim had stripped the canvas of the faux Messina, revealing a startling vision of a crucifixion. The surreal vision was unlike anything Bernard or Armand had ever seen.

Armand stepped closer to inspect the unknown artist's brushstrokes and technique. "At first glance, Bernie, I thought it might be a Dali, since the famous old Spaniard painted a series of religious works back in the fifties. But the technique is different."

Bernard grimaced. "Well, you would certainly know better than I, Armand. Modern art is not my forte."

"Nor is it mine, Bernie. Most of my experience and  training had come from my father, when I lived in Florence and visited him at the *Uffizi*. But I have always been drawn to the surrealists and have examined many works over the years, so I can say quite confidently this crucifixion is not by Dali. But since Dali is still alive, perhaps we could ask him if he knows who this surrealist artist might be."

"I must say," Bernard said as his eyes scanned the canvas, "despite not being acquainted with surrealism, this version is quite stunning."

Armand gazed back at the tall, elongated canvas, which stood four-feet tall and two-feet wide. "It is rather dramatic, and akin to Dali's great masterwork of the same subject, even if Dali's technical prowess is superior." Armand studied the work for several moments, then added, "However, this composition conveys some very profound spiritual concepts that other crucifixions don't."

As they both stared at the mysterious work, they realized that the painting at first shocked the viewer with an unnatural sense of melodrama, yet the fantastical vision was clearly not intended to be a realistic portrayal of Jesus at

Golgotha. Rather it was deeply symbolic with religious import.

The gargantuan cross, which towers over two other crucifixions of condemned souls, stood in a fog-laden valley, as the dark, cloudy sky parted to shed light on Jesus. Meanwhile, Jesus' colossal cross stood perfectly straight and true—unlike those of the two mortals beside him—and towered majestically above mankind, symbolically residing in the heavens, while mankind resided in the lower earthly realm, with craggy rocks and rough terrain; symbolic of the travails that mankind must endure in a precarious world.

Moreover, the convict that Jesus had absolved of sin was placed at his front, in partial light, while the other eternally damned soul resided at Jesus' back, in the shadows. What remained quite clear, however, was that the intense focal point of the divine drama was unquestionably Jesus. Hence, amid the dark and turbulent veil of clouds, which fittingly bemoaned the fateful event, God the Father's divine light miraculously parted the heavens to warmly embrace His son.

"A stunning work, indeed," Bernard said. "It's a Divine Crucifixion in every sense. But not knowing who this mysterious artist is, or was, leaves me in a most precarious position, Armand."

Armand turned and surveyed the room. "You said you purchased three other works recently. Were they from the same seller?"

"Yes, I bought them from Michel Tucci. He is an Italian fellow, fairly well known in the industry. How could he not be, he's ninety years old."

"Ninety!?" Armand nearly choked. "He's almost as old as Messina."

Bernard chuckled, then smirked. "Yes, Michel has been around for almost a century, but in retrospect, he hasn't sold that many paintings. And all of those transactions were in Europe. Nevertheless, he established a good reputation, so we felt confident in our purchase, especially since all the exposed rears of the canvases were tested as being authentic in age. Quite distressing, however, is that I tried calling Mr. Tucci, but his landlord answered. He said Michel had unexpectedly moved, without saying a word or leaving a forwarding address. He's vanished."

Armand squinted. "Hmm, I never heard of this Michel Tucci. But my father knows many contacts throughout Europe, so I'm confident he or someone he knows must have crossed paths with Signore Tucci."

"My thoughts, exactly, Armand."

"But first, we should inspect those three other acquisitions of yours, as I suspect they might be forgeries, as well."

Barnard recoiled with a shiver. "Good grief! I certainly hope not. A quarter of a million dollars lost thus far is more than enough for my weak heart to endure."

"Well, it's best if you face the grim reality now, Bernie, so we can make plans as to how to solve this mysterious crime."

Bernard instructed his technician to X-ray the three remaining pieces, being that the machine had been broken for two months and was recently repaired. Bernard and Armand both held their breath as the machine snapped the three films and the technician developed the X-rays. To Bernard's poor-old-heart's despair, all three indicated that surreal images existed underneath. Bernard then instructed Jim to strip the canvases by removing the top veneer of paint. However, as Jim stripped the last painting, Bernard and Armand shrieked, "Eureka!" and "Bingo!" respectively, when it revealed a very special clue. It was signed!

Armand smiled. "Well, Bernie, at least now we know the name of our mysterious modern artist."

Bernard shrugged. "Yes, but who the hell is Paolo Santanello?"

"Don't know. Never heard of him. I'll have to make some inquires. But it still doesn't explain who the nefarious forger is." Armand shook his head, baffled. "And why did the forger use Santanello's works of art to paint his fakes?" Armand crossed his muscular arms as he pondered the enigma further. "Perhaps he's a rival or an enemy of Paolo's. Or possibly he simply purchased these unknown paintings and decided to use them for his criminal charade." He shook his head. "None of this makes much sense."

Bernard paused in thought, then said, "I just wonder if Michel Tucci knew if these were fakes, or if he was hoodwinked by the forger, as well?"

"Yes, there are several possible explanations, Bernie, but there's only one way to find out. It's time for me to seriously start my investigation."

Bernard sighed with a modicum of relief, knowing well Armand Arnolfini's impressive record for success. "So, what will be your first course of action?"

"I plan on catching a flight to Florence, Italy, to visit my dad. I sense this Michel Tucci fellow returned home and, as mentioned, my father has many connections in Italy and throughout Europe. What's more, the timing is right, as I'm overdue to see my Pa anyhow. Like Signore Tucci, he, too, is an old man. So, two birds, one stone, as they say."

Before catching his flight, Armand thumbed through his Rolodex and managed to contact Salvador Dali. He hoped the old master might know who Paolo Santanello might be, perhaps being a minor surrealist from the early years of the genre's birth. But the great Dali had no recollection of an artist by that name.

Armand then caught his flight on Alitalia and landed in Florence. He hopped on a rented Vespa and traveled over the Ponte Vecchio, past the Pitti Palace, and turned down the excruciatingly narrow Via Toscanella, where he arrived at his father's midsized but exquisite apartment. His father, Sergio, took almost two minutes to answer the door, but when he did, father and son embraced, warmly, lovingly.

"So good to see you, my son," Sergio said with a gracious smile that stretched across his wrinkled yet still handsome face. "What brings you home to Florence, work or pleasure?"

Armand smiled, with a touch of regret. "Well, both, Papa. But to be honest, work has lured me back, this time to a mysterious art crime, a forgery. Rather, four forgeries: one of the Renaissance master Messina, and three lesser-known artists from the same era, including Domenico Alfani, Antonio Boselli and Domenico Panetti."

Sergio's eighty-year-old eyes ignited with a sparkle, one not seen in many years. "Ah! How I miss being engaged in the passionate world of art, even if dealing with forgeries." He scratched his well-groomed head of gray hair with his wrinkled hand, which was adorned with a stunning Cellini-like golden ring, then slipped on his immaculately tailored, designer dinner jacket. "But I wonder why this forger chooses relatively obscure Renaissance artists. Surely they don't fetch anywhere near the price of a Raphael or a Titian, and the painstaking work that goes into these works is extremely intricate and time-consuming."

Armand walked over to the refrigerator and pulled out a Peroni. He extended it to his dad, who refused, and he popped off the top. He took a swig and savored the smooth barley malt flavor as it titillated his palate. With a swish of his tongue and a pucker of his lips, he swallowed, then said, "Good question, Pa. But I'm more interested in finding out who this forger is, because there's an additional mystery to this case; namely, all his forgeries are painted over the works of the same surrealist artist, a guy named Paolo Santanello. Have you ever heard of him? Or an art dealer named Michel Tucci?"

Sergio squinted as his mind took several attempts to start up, like an old gas-powered generator being started with a pull-string. After a few blinks, his eyes began to glow. "Yes, yes! I vaguely recall a Signore Tucci. He was a small-time dealer of lesser-known artists, like the ones you mentioned, but nothing in particular or nefarious stands out about him. And this Santanello fella doesn't ring a bell, Armand. I'm sorry." He paused and rubbed his temple as a distant memory began to materialize in the dark and dusty abyss of his antiquated mind. He gazed at the wall, then up at the ceiling. His eyes oscillated, looking everywhere, yet nowhere in particular.

Armand put his bottle of beer down. "What is it, Pop?"

Sergio's wandering eyes suddenly stopped, then gazed at his son. "Ah! Yes, of course. I do recall a strange occurrence, it happened many years ago. I believe it was nineteen fifty-four, or was it five? Hmm, no, I think it was—"

"Never mind the date, Pop, what was it you remember?"

Sergio was bumped out of his data-seeking rut like a needle skipping on an LP, and he got back on track. He blinked hard and nodded with a smile of gratification, happy to have remembered something from his distant past. The biggest bane of his life was the slow and humiliating loss of his precious knowledge and memories. He grasped the lapel of his stylish jacket and boldly declared, "Clara, Clara Vandermeer."

Armand stifled a chuckle. "Yes, that's just splendid, Pa. That's a very nice name. But what about Clara Vandermeer?"

Sergio teasingly paused, then with a proud smile, said, "Clara happens to be the curator of the *Groeninge Museum* in Bruges, Belgium. It houses a fine selection of Northern Renaissance masters and several surreal works, including one by René Magritte." As Armand's eyes widened, Sergio added, "However, Clara had experienced some sort of incident when she started her surrealist collection, but I can't for the life of me recall what it was. Nevertheless, with her keen knowledge of Renaissance and modern surrealist works, I imagine she could be very helpful in your quest."

"Indeed she can!" Armand said with a warm grin. "I knew I could count on you, Papa. *Grazie!*"

"*Prego*," Sergio replied. Yet his prideful face soon withered. "Does that mean you're leaving me already?"

Armand grasped his bottle of Peroni and took a short sip, his smile morphing into a solemn portrait of regret. "Well, I'll spend two days here with you, Pa, but unfortunately work beckons me, as it did you for so many years. I'm sure you can understand the magnetism of doing something you love."

Sergio glanced at his prized collection of high-quality lithograph reproductions, featuring several masterpieces from the Renaissance and Baroque eras, then back at his ambitious son. "Very true, my boy, very true. Who am I to clip your wings when I soared with the greatest names in Renaissance art for so many years at the *Uffizi Gallery*, and had the good fortune of teaching that wealth of knowledge and culture to several younger generations?"

Armand lovingly wrapped his arm around his father and walked him up the spiral staircase to the top floor of the apartment. There they gazed out of a large picture window, as their line of sight traveled across the Arno River to see the splendid vista of the city of Florence, the cultural epicenter of the Renaissance with the majestic Il Duomo, along with the *Uffizi Gallery* and art academy where Sergio took much pride in Florence's rich past, a lifetime spent preserving a critical milestone of Western civilization.

Moments later they strolled down to the kitchen, where, together, they cooked a savory meal of hot antipasto, raviolis, and eggplant rollatini. They reminisced about their early days, when Armand lived in Florence, from his birth to the time he played for AC Milan, as well as sharing loving memories of Armand's dear mother, who had died of polio when Armand was only thirteen. Afterwards, they capped the night off with cappuccino and homemade tiramisu, Armand's favorite dessert, and bid each other good night.

Two days later, Armand arrived at the *Groeninge Museum* in Bruges.

Clara approached him, wearing a stylish full-length dress and her gray hair pulled back in a bun. Her physique and skin didn't betray the fact that she was seventy-eight years old, as she said, "Welcome, Signore Arnolfini. Your father apprised me of your desire to speak with me, yet did not mention the topic of your interest. How can I help you?"

Armand's eyes, however, were drawn to the painting behind her, as he cordially shook her hand and said, "Excuse me, Mrs. Vandermeer, but I must see your *Portrait of Margareta van Eyck.*"

Clara smiled; being used to men being drawn away by Jan van Eyck's masterful works. She had long ago resigned herself to taking second fiddle, as she graciously turned and pointed to the larger painting beside the famous portrait. "And that's van Eyck's second largest surviving panel, after his illustrious *Ghent Altarpiece*. It is the *Virgin and Child with Saints Donatian and George and—*"

"They're both magnificent!" Armand interjected, as he stepped closer, his eyes devouring them as if the tiramisu he had eaten two nights before. "I've always had an affinity for Jan van Eyck's work. Perhaps it's because my great, great ancestor was immortalized in his most famous painting."

Clara's head recoiled. "You're not saying you're related to Giovanni Arnolfini, are you? Certainly you jest."

"Why do you say that?"

Clara looked at Armand with reproachful eyes. "Because I had asked your father about that many years ago, and he said you were not related."

Armand chuckled. "Yes, my father can be very critical, as I'm sure you're well aware. It's his highly perceptive yet merciless eye as an art critic that had jaded him to van Eyck's masterpiece."

Clara squinted. "What's not to like?"

"Well, he whole-heartedly admires van Eyck's technical prowess, being perhaps the greatest technician of the Renaissance. Moreover, Jan's attention to detail and his precision of painting inert objects was second to none. However, my father abhorred many of van Eyck's figures, and of Giovanni in particular. He said our great ancestor did *not* look like a rigid corpse, or an ugly porcelain doll, and took it as a personal affront to our great Arnolfini name."

Clara's lips parted with a reflective smile. "That does sound like you father. Sergio was always a most brilliant and knowledgeable man, but aesthetics dominated his every decision."

Armand nodded. "Yes, but while I can be just as critical, I can also overlook human flaws to recognize a masterpiece in overall execution. The composition and technique of the *Arnolfini Portrait* is absolutely stunning, especially considering it was painted in fourteen thirty-four, some eighteen years before da Vinci was even born."

"You are absolutely correct, Signore Arnolfini. But I'm sure you didn't come all the way to Belgium just to tell me of your famous relation to a Flemish masterpiece."

Armand chuckled. "No, not at all. I've come on business. I'm investigating a case for Bernard Higley at the *Cloisters Museum*." As Clara nodded, acknowledging her acquaintance with the American curator, Armand continued, "He recently acquired four works by Italian Renaissance artists. However, all four were forgeries. More peculiar still, all four were painted over the works of a modern surrealist artist."

Clara gasped. "How awful! Poor Bernard."

Armand scanned the gallery as he inquired, "My father said you have an eye for old Renaissance masters and modern surrealists. Have you ever purchased works from a man by the name of Michel Tucci?"

Clara's eyes at first squinted, then opened wide. "Yes! In fact I did. I believe it was back in nineteen fifty-five."

Clara went on to explain how Michel Tucci had originally approached her attempting to sell the works of an unknown surrealist artist. Despite her interest in surrealism—even purchasing a Magritte, among others—Clara had refused Michel's offer, being that she wasn't in the market for unknown artists. However, a year later, Tucci returned, this time offering a splendid array of Flemish, German, Italian, and French artists from the Renaissance to Rococo eras. And despite those artists being lesser known, they were not *unknown*, and well worth the reasonable investment.

Armand's jaw twisted as his mind reeled. "Would you mind if I take a look at those acquisitions?"

"Of course not. Come, right this way."

As they entered another gallery, Clara pointed to six paintings. "Here they are." Her face was now marred with concern. "You're not suggesting that Michel sold me fakes, as well, are you?"

"It's a distinct possibility, Mrs. Vandermeer. I think it would be wise to have them X-rayed to see if they're forgeries."

Clara grimaced. "The mere thought of this makes me ill, Signore Arnolfini. We no longer have an X-ray machine, but I'll have an infrared reflectogram done. It's also noninvasive and will determine what exactly lies underneath the top layer of paint. And I'm hoping it's nothing more than base pigment."

An hour later, Armand and Clara found themselves in a back room, waiting impatiently as the technician scanned the works. The first one proved to be an original, but as the remaining five were scanned, they each revealed a painting underneath. Clara and Armand gasped, especially since all five appeared to be in the same style as the mysterious, surrealist artist Paolo Santanello.

Clara's face turned crimson red as she spat, "Where is this Michel Tucci!?"

Armand gazed solemnly at the paintings, then back at Clara. "I have no idea. I was hoping you might have some insights as to where he might be. I know he lived somewhere in Italy, but his last known whereabouts was in the United States, when he sold Bernard Higley those forgeries. Yet, when Bernard tried to contact him, his landlord said he had moved, with no forwarding address."

Clara glanced at the five fakes and grunted. "You can have them, they're worthless!"

Armand twitched. "I'm truly sorry for revealing this scam, Mrs. Vandermeer. I can only imagine how upset you must be. However, while I appreciate your offer, I couldn't possibly take them."

Clara shook her head and slammed the table. "Upset doesn't begin to explain how humiliated and deceived I feel! Michel Tucci seemed like a nice respectable man, and I knew of several other curators who had purchased works from him, as well." She paused, then added, "Yet, I have not heard a word about him for many years, until this recent scam you've just mentioned at the *Cloisters*. Do you have any idea if Tucci knows these works are fakes, or is he being duped like us?"

"That's a good question, Mrs. Vandermeer, one that we've been asking, as well. But I aim to find out."

No sooner did he finish that sentence, than Clara's secretary entered the room. "Mrs. Vandermeer, there is an urgent phone call for you from a Mister Sergio Arnolfini. He wishes to speak to his son." Peering over Clara's shoulder, she added, "Is that him?"

Armand stepped briskly into view, fearing his father might be ill. "Yes, I'm his son. Where is the phone?"

Armand dashed to the main office and picked up the receiver. "Pop, what's wrong? Are you okay?"

Sergio's voice surged through the earpiece, "I'm fine, Armand. However, my dear friend, Anton Platzer, just called me. He's the curator at the Schwarzenberg Palace, in Prague. And get this, he just discovered that two recent acquisitions were revealed as forgeries!"

An electric chill ran down Armand's back. "Don't tell me, Michel Tucci was the dealer and Anton found surreal paintings underneath?"

"Exactly, Armand. Evidently, Tucci's fakes have spread like a virus."

Armand wrapped up his conversation with his father, then bid Clara farewell. Taking another flight, Armand landed in Czechoslovakia, and dashed to the Schwarzenberg Palace.

Anton Platzer greeted Armand with open arms and a broken heart. He explained how he had purchased the works of two minor artists: Hans von Aachen, a German painter of Northern Mannerism, and Norbert Grund, a painter of the Rococo style from Prague.

Armand examined the works, marveling over the skill and detail of the disparate styles of the forgeries, yet remained baffled about the forger's reason for painting over another artist's work. *Who would do such a thing, and why?* He thought.

"Mr. Platzer, my father informed me that you purchased these paintings from Michel Tucci, is that correct?"

"Yes. I can't believe that feeble old man sold me fakes," Anton huffed. "He seemed so sincere and kind. Not to mention that his sterling reputation had preceded him."

Armand glanced at the two paintings. "Do you have any idea where Tucci might be?"

"All I know is that he moved to the United States. I believe he is somewhere in New York."

"Are you sure he didn't move back home to Italy? He recently made a score in New York at the *Cloisters Museum* and abandoned his apartment."

Anton shook his head. "No, I believe his trail here in Europe is too well worn and beginning to fall apart for him to remain here. It appears he is now staking out new territory." He scratched his head. "But does Tucci know that he's selling fakes, or is he just a blind fool, like all of us?"

"My guess is that he knows very well what he's doing. That all of his forgeries are painted over the same artist's works seems to indicate he or his forger knew this artist and didn't care much for his modernist bent. So either he or someone he knows covered them over with very skillful renditions of old masters, and he's making a pretty penny in the process."

"A pretty *penny*! Huh! That scoundrel fleeced me of fifty thousand dollars. And I hear Clara and Bernard, among others, have all lost more than that. I'll gladly contribute five thousand dollars to your investigation if you catch this despicable old weasel."

"Thank you, I aim to try, Mr. Platzer. I'll be in touch." Armand shook his hand and took his leave.

Catching a flight to JFK airport, Armand returned to his apartment on the Upper East Side, several blocks from the *Metropolitan Museum of Art* and the *Guggenheim*. As he sat on the couch watching an episode of *The Rockford Files*, his mind wandered. *If Michel Tucci came to America*, he thought, *he didn't come empty handed!*

He zapped the TV off with the remote, then called Peter Hansen, an old friend in the FBI. He asked Peter to scan all the manifests of air and sea freight shipments from Italy containing the name Michel Tucci. Peter obliged, and three hours later, Armand's phone rang.

"Hello? Peter?"

"Yeah, Arnolfini. It's Saint Peter. I came through for you. Your pal Michel had a large shipment made from Italy last year. Manifest number 83290. It was then delivered to an address in upstate New York on February third." Peter paused, then added, "I actually bought some property up in Wurtsboro. It's beautiful and peaceful, Arnolfini. You know, getting away from the rat race and all. Kind of like Green Acres." Peter then began singing the jingle, "Greeeen Acres is the place to be. Faaaarm livin' is the life for—"

"For Pete's sake, Pete! Stop clowning around! What's the address?"

Peter chuckled. "Okay, hold your piglets, Arnol... Ziffel."

"Don't be a ham, Pete! Because if you were, you'd have botulism."

Peter laughed, then snorted as he said, "Okay, okay, it was delivered to 157 Highview Terrace in Bloomingburg, New York. Do you need the zip code, too, Arnolfini?"

"No, that will do. I owe you one, Pete!"

"One?" Peter said. "How about a hundred and one!"

"Well, if you really want to start counting, I guess you'd have to sell your house in Brookville to pay *me* back."

Peter chuckled. "Very true, Arnolfini. You know I'm toying with ya. But you really should come up and see my property in Green Acres. There's a guy up there who, I swear, looks just like Mr. Haney. In fact, I think it *is* Mr, Haney!"

Armand finally laughed. "You're a knucklehead, Pete. But, okay, we'll have to hook up for dinner one day and checkout your property. But I have to run. This lead is a good one. Thanks again!"

Armand hopped in his brand new '79 gold Oldsmobile Toronado, which was released three months prior to the New Year, and turned on the radio. It was playing *Runnin' with the Devil* by a new band called Van Halen. Armand smirked as he thought how Michel Tucci was also running with the Devil. He then tuned in WQXR. He smiled; it was playing Franz Liszt's revolutionary *Second Piano Concerto*, a twenty-two-minute masterpiece of pure genius. He slammed the car into gear and headed upstate on the New York Thruway.

He crossed over the Tappan Zee Bridge, past the Ramapo rest stop, and headed west at Exit 16. Before long he came to Exit 114, then drove up the winding street, onto Highview Terrace, which eventually reached the peak of the mountain. As he gazed out, he was overcome by the lush panorama of the Hudson Valley, which spread out as far as the eye could see in all directions, with distant mountains sculpting the horizon.

What a spot! He thought. *A spot anyone would relish, especially an art dealer.* He chuckled. *Or even Mr. Haney.*

As he drove farther along the dirt country road, he came upon a startling sight, a towering A-frame chalet that stood majestically on the summit.

Armand scanned the area; there wasn't another house or person in sight. He turned off the engine and stepped out. The silence, seclusion, and sky-scraping perch atop the highest peak in the valley struck him at once as quite eerie, yet sublimely ethereal. Now he understood why people called areas like this God's Country. The Shawangunk Mountain Range had a special charm all its own.

As the thick cumulus clouds in the distance parted, a beam of sunlight shed its golden rays upon the valley and onto the tiny telephone poles below, which suddenly appeared like small crucifixes. The image of Santanello's surreal crucifixion came streaming back into his consciousness. Armand shook his head free of the mirage and walked up to the modern chalet. Gazing up at the peculiar, stylish structure, Armand was moved by the pyramidal shape that was so prominent in houses of worship or the grand pyramids of Egypt. He was expecting to find an unassuming hideout, certainly nothing like *this*.

He walked up the broad redwood deck and up to the large glass sliding doors. He rang the bell and waited.

No response.

He shifted from side to side, to see if he could peer through the curtains, but to no avail. He knocked on the glass door, but that too yielded no reaction.

Disheartened, Armand returned to his Toronado and drove down the mountain, making his way to the Shawanga Lodge. He rented a room and had a meal in the motel's restaurant, which fell drastically short of pleasing his cultivated palate. With his appetite at least satiated, he watched an episode of *Barney Miller*, then retired for the night.

Early the next morning, Armand drove back up to the A-frame chalet. As he approached the peak of the mountain, he slowed down. Parked on the gravel driveway was a yellow, Supercharged 1937 Cord 812 Coupe. He pulled up alongside the rare and precious automobile, with its distinctive flex-chrome exhaust pipes, and came to a stop. He gazed at the quarter-million-dollar car and shook his head, irritated: *And they say crime doesn't pay. Ha!*

He slid out of his Oldsmobile and climbed quietly up the deck and reached the sliding doors. Once again, he couldn't see past the sheer curtains to decipher Michel Tucci or any moving silhouette. He rang the bell.

Nothing.

He knocked on the glass doors.

Again, nothing.

Armand sighed as he dejectedly gazed at the ground, his mind reeling: *Where did the old swindler go? Or is the decrepit old crook just deaf?* He turned right and looked at the radiant '37 Cord. *The old geezer certainly has good taste though.*

On instinct, Armand turned left, where the glare from a patch of white birch trees reflected into his eyes. As he squinted, he noticed the dense woods had a narrow path. It lured him in. As he strolled through the tall columns of trees, with their smooth and almost magically glistening bark, Armand eventually came upon a clearing. He stopped dead in his tracks!

Up ahead he saw an old man sitting at an easel, painting a mysteriously somber yet beautiful landscape. There was no mistaking it; the enigmatic canvas was in every sense the work of Jacob van Ruisdael, the 17th century Dutch master.

Silently, Armand walked up behind him and gazed down at the painting. "That's rather intriguing."

Michel jolted, then turned, shock marring his wrinkled face, as Armand wryly added, "It looks exactly like Jacob van Ruisdael's *Jewish Cemetery*, especially since I see no cemeteries or ruins in the Hudson Valley from here."

"You have quite an eye for the old masters, Mr.—?"

"Arnolfini, Armand Arnolfini."

"Arnolfini?" Michel queried in his thick Italian accent. "As in Jan van Eyck's *Giovanni Arnolfini?*"

"The very same, indeed, just several generations removed."

"My Lord, son. You come from a mighty famous family. Yet, I must confess, you look nothing like your ancestor, and thank heavens for that! You look rather healthy and alive."

"Yes, and my vision and sense of deduction is also quite healthy," Armand said as he glanced back at the canvas. "Do you intend to sign that Jacob van Ruisdael?"

Michel laughed. "You may be a famous Arnolfini, Armand, but I am not a van Ruisdael. Nor a Jacob, at that. I am just a nobody."

Armand smiled. "You are certainly not a nobody, Paolo."

Michel's lips twisted with confusion. "What do you mean by Paolo? My name is Michel, Michel Tucci."

"Nice try. But you, signore, are Paolo Santanello—a phenomenal surrealist artist who, for some reason, remains an enigma."

Michel laughed, mockingly. "You, son, have a vivid imagination. How ever did you deduce such a fallacy?"

"I'm sure the names Bernard Higley, Clara Vandermeer, and Anton Platzer ring a few bells." Michel rolled his eyes, unimpressed, as Armand continued, "And quite oddly, Franz Liszt's *Second Piano Concerto* also aided in my deduction."

Michel's head recoiled, now totally confused. "A concerto!?" He then snickered with a condescending smile as he shook his head and slapped his leg. "You are most entertaining, Signore Arnolfini. But, please, do explain."

Armand remained stern and stoic. "Well, you see, Liszt had pioneered a very unique device. He launched his concerto with a single theme, which then underwent a series of transformations, at one point dark and brooding, and other times playful, dreamy, or even triumphant, but all emanating from that same single kernel. It made me realize that all these various old masterworks, which appeared to be by different Renaissance artists, were all by the same hand, the hand of a modern surrealist whose tantalizing works appeared underneath all of them. You, Paolo, are the kernel, the one theme that carried through the entire set, being brilliantly transformed only on the surface by masterful forgeries." Armand cracked a satiated smile as he peered deeply into the phantom forger's eyes. "So after contemplating all those loose ends, and now seeing you paint this picture, your name alone, Signore Santanello, ties them all together."

Paolo's frail shoulders wilted as his gnarly old hand laid the paintbrush down near his rich palette of oils. He expelled a sigh of regret mixed with relief. "It's been a long hard road, son, and I'm at the end of that trail. Life isn't always fair." His eyes veered toward the canvas then back up at Armand. "It has long been said that hard work and effort will reap great rewards. But I say, *bah!*" Paolo blustered with cynicism. "I had studied with intense vigor, Signore Arnolfini, perfecting my craft to the highest degree possible, yet met with one rejection after another by curators, snobs, and collectors of all sorts. I'll have you know, as a young lad, back in the early nineteen hundreds, I had created startling images of surrealism, even before those of Giorgio de Chirico. His now famous painting *Song of Love* had allegedly ignited the avant-garde genre of surrealism in nineteen fourteen, some ten years before André Breton *allegedly* founded the movement." Paolo shook his head with disgust. "How bizarre and flawed mankind is in documenting progress or ascribing credit."

Armand nodded, knowing well the flaws of recorded history. "I must admit, Paolo, although I have a personal interest in surrealism, my father and I have long been aficionados of the old masters, so my knowledge of surrealism's founding is not clear." Armand squinted. "But are you saying you actually pioneered surrealism before de Chirico?"

Paolo snickered. "My boy, as I said, life is not fair. Yes, I *did*. As a young man in nineteen eleven, at age twenty-two, my work was on display in an open market in Turin, Italy, my hometown. By an odd stroke of bad luck, Giorgio de Chirico happened to pass through my village on his way to Paris. Some three years later, I had seen a photo of *Song of Love* in a newspaper article, heralding de Chirico as a pioneer. That work—might I add—was very much like the one I had on display three years prior. Oh, yes, Signore Arnolfini, I most certainly pioneered surrealism well before de Chirico, Dali, Ernst, Magritte, and the rest."

"I don't understand," Armand said. "If Giorgio and others were breaking new ground with their art, why did your attempts fail? Especially if your artwork was not only similar but the precursor."

Paolo swallowed hard as his wrinkled lips twisted. He looked up at Armand, his weathered and once vibrant brown eyes now reduced to two black pools of pain and sorrow. "My father had died in the Great War, and my mother's health spiraled into a deep state of melancholy. It was either abandon her and strike out into the world for self glory or retreat back into the womb of my existence, namely the warm and tender-loving arms of my mother."

Solemnly, Armand shook his head as his eyes drifted to the vast panorama of mountains and streams in the Hudson Valley, then back at Paolo's improvised van Ruisdael. "I'm still a bit baffled, Paolo. You have extraordinary talents. This van Ruisdael is just as magnificent as the other artists you copied with masterful skill, each in different genres no less. You mean to say you couldn't score a big hit, somehow?"

Paolo began packing up his materials as he said, "Armand, technical skills of imitation are not worth a damn. What makes a great artist great is their heart and soul, imagination and innovation. Anyone can acquire a wealth of knowledge, yet only those who utilize that knowledge in a unique and innovative fashion have earned the right to be called brilliant. These forgeries I have done over the years have all been cheap imitations. Painting restorers are a dime a dozen, and their names remain obscured and their financial rewards remain marginal. And in a sense, rightfully so. I missed my chance when I was young to make my mark. My mother lived for twenty more years after my father died, yet by that time World War Two had broken out and the world was not interested in buying art, as much of it was hidden or stolen. Especially by that fat bastard Hermann Goering! He was the world's biggest art thief."

Paolo stood up and folded his chair as he continued, "Fortune has not shone upon me in regard to my art, but did so with my heart. Those years with my mother, and the woman who had become my wife, were the pearls in the oyster shell that became my sheltered life. When they both died in a Fascist raid by Mussolini's henchmen, that's when I myself spiraled into a sad state of depression. It crippled me for a decade, until I decided to paint over my own creative canvases with forgeries of old masters to make a living, a *fair* living, one more in line financially with my worth. Great artists, Signore Arnolfini, deserve adequate compensation for the rich cultural enhancements they bequeath to civilization. Over countless centuries too many great artists, musicians, and even inventors have died penniless and forgotten, yet mankind has not made any attempts to correct this most humiliating and debilitating flaw."

Paolo cleaned his paintbrush carefully with turpentine and packed it neatly away with his linseed oil and special varnishes, as he added, "I have chosen to forge the works of lesser-known artists to keep a low profile and not incite a world-wide manhunt." He paused but a moment, then said reflectively, "However, I suppose I sold my soul to the devil, burying my love and passion under a veneer of falsehoods just to earn a fair living. Now I am ninety years old and the journey is almost over. Soon I shall cross the celestial threshold and return to my loving wife and mother's arms, and get to see my father once again."

Paolo handed Armand the painting and folding chair and collected his easel and paints. "Come, follow me."

They travelled back through the glaring birch trees and returned to Santanello's unique A-frame chalet, with his exquisite '37 Cord parked in the driveway.

Armand stopped. "Ah, yes. Now it all fits." He glanced at the priceless old Cord, then up at the modern chalet. "You cherish antiquity, but also modernity."

Paolo chuckled. "Very good, Armand. Yes, I most certainly do. I admire the old masters, but progress must be made. In fact, if you're wondering where I got all the old canvas fabric to paint my modern artwork, it was from my ancestor who owned a mill during the Renaissance. I had found reams of it in his attic and thought it would be interesting to paint modern visions on ancient canvas. Only later, when I began my charade, did I realize that my forgeries would be readily accepted when they examined the canvas from the back. Odd, how that, too, all worked out, as if destiny tried to throw me one small bone. But now it's over. *Finito.* So, please, follow me."

As they entered the chalet, Armand's eyes illuminated. There before him was a sprawling arrangement of paintings of all sizes by various artists, famous artists. Armand placed the faux van Ruisdael and folding-chair down and stepped closer to inspect *Aristotle Contemplating the Bust of Homer* by Rembrandt. He marveled over the light and dark brushstrokes that precisely imitated the great Dutch master. Then he stepped over and gazed at *The Crucifixion of Saint Peter* by Caravaggio. He stepped back and said, "Dear God, Paolo! I have studied the originals up close many times, and I must say, these are fantastic. I cannot tell the difference." He glanced at Paolo. "It's scary how mind-boggling your skills are. You have masterfully reproduced the works of two great titans who shared a very similar style."

Paolo approached Armand's side. "Yes, as I said, life is not always fair. For many years Rembrandt basked in the limelight because of his dramatic style of chiaroscuro, while

Caravaggio—being the true pioneer of the style—remained in the shadows, forgotten for centuries. It's a crime to humanity." Paolo paused, then added, "Actually, in an odd way, it's sadly apropos, as their painterly style of light and shadow underscored their own disparate fates." He gazed up at Armand. "Wouldn't you agree?"

Armand shrugged. "Well, yes. But in recent years there's been a revival of Caravaggio's works. And now both great masters share the limelight. So, you see, Paolo, life sometimes corrects its mistakes, even if years or centuries later. After all, Mozart died and was buried in a pauper's grave. He, too, had fallen into obscurity for many years, having been blotted out by the huge shadow of Antonio Salieri. Yet Wolfgang rose from the ashes, like a phoenix, and has now cast Salieri into the shadows. So, genius often has a way of rising to the top."

Paolo's brief smile of acknowledgement turned into a frown. "Yes, but that some geniuses had to wait years or a century to be rediscovered is an awful tragedy. And who knows how many more Mozarts and Caravaggios have existed over time who will never see the light? There is much darkness in this world, much of which is borne in ignorance or sheer stupidity."

Armand stood silent and pensive, until several other canvases drew his attention; one by Renoir, another by Magritte, and still another by Holbein. "I thought you said you only painted forgeries of lesser-known artists?"

Paolo chuckled. "Well, these are copies of paintings I personally adore. I never had intentions of selling *them*."

Armand examined them closer. "Are all of these painted over original creations of yours?"

Paolo's smile withered. "Yes. I suppose in a state of self-loathing, regret, or perhaps disgust, I have embarked on erasing myself from this cruel and unfair world." He gazed down at the van Ruisdael leaning against the wall. He expelled a deep breath, taking comfort in its significance, for the wet veneer of paint was slowly hardening, thus suffocating the last breath of the unknown surrealist underneath. "That is my swan song, Signore Arnolfini. I aptly chose van Ruisdael's gloomy landscape with a cemetery to vanquish my work, and inter my very self. I am now officially obscured from the eyes and minds of the unjust, the cliquey elites, the snobby academics, and the unfortunate public that shall never have a chance to judge my works for themselves." Paolo handed Armand a document that he had filled in while Armand was inspecting his collection.

Armand looked down and began to read it, when his eyes widened. His head snapped up, but it was too late, Paolo choked, wobbled, and collapsed.

Armand dropped the document and hurriedly knelt down by Paolo's side. Concernedly, he lifted the frail old man's head. His boney neck felt as if it might break, while his thin layer of skin seemed as if it might tear. "Paolo!" Armand cried as his heart raced. "Can you hear me?"

Paolo's eyes opened half way as he coughed and gurgled, while a rivulet of blood coursed down the side of his mouth. "Armand, I've managed to beat lung cancer for almost a year, but it's over. I have no family left. And who better to make the executor of all my wealth than an Arnolfini—a man with deep roots to a glorious artistic past. It appears destiny has brought you here, in this... final...hour, this...final—"

A painful lump welled in Armand's throat as he could feel the old man's body wilt and begin to stiffen—the warmth of a near century-long life slowly dissipating, as it ebbed into the cold abyss of death.

A tear welled in Armand's eye as he sat speechless, gazing at the old artist, then peering at the gallery of pseudo old masterpieces that extinguished a genuinely great, but unknown, modern artist.

Armand leaned back and once again gazed at Paolo's will. Not only did Paolo authorize Armand to be his executor, but Santanello had also left several millions of dollars to be dispersed to numerous art academies, which would be awarded as scholarships to promising young talents; budding artistic geniuses who exhibit the prospect of uplifting civilization in one form or another.

Once again Armand peered down at the mysterious phantom forger in his arms. He had vigorously hunted him down with contempt, only to find himself saddened and burdened with a heavy heart and conflicting thoughts. The dead old man before him was clearly a genius in his own right, but by the twisted forces of fate had been dealt a bad set of celestial cards. His mission of gaining financial compensation was not borne out of self-interest or greed, but rather a philanthropic endeavor to right the injustice of an often cruel and imperfect world, a world that routinely overshadowed or even trampled over many with extraordinary talent, either due to roadblocks by haughty elites, a lack of connections, a depletion of profits by greedy capitalists, or simply bad karma.

That Santanello had also made a life-long decision to literally erase his art, and in essence himself, from the world of art also struck Armand hard. A tear unexpectedly escaped from his eye and streamed down his solemn face. Yet as he gazed up at all of Paolo's forgeries, and contemplated all the press his monumental crime would soon engender, another thought struck him: will Santanello's surreal under-paintings now be revealed, thus being his passport into the pantheon of the ironclad-world of Fine Art?

Armand Arnolfini wiped the tear from his eye, and smiled.

The Russian Link

Armand Arnolfini's yellow 1937 Cord Coupe purred as he drove down Madison Avenue. He had inherited the classic quarter-million-dollar automobile from Paolo Santanello two years earlier, in 1978, after Armand had solved the now famous Phantom Forger case. Oddly enough, after Santanello's death, his surreal artwork had hit the world by storm, catapulting his name into the ranks of Dali, Magritte and the ultimate masters of surrealism, with his works fetching tens of millions of dollars or more at Christie's and Sotheby's. Beyond the exotic car, Santanello's estate entitled Armand to a five-percent royalty for the sale of Paolo's artwork; hence Armand's financial situation had been significantly augmented.

Arnolfini's notoriety of being a top-notch private investigator had also escalated since then, but it was now Sunday evening and his day to relax. As he made a hard right onto 57th Street, he ejected his cassette of Pink Floyd's new double album *The Wall*. As he came to a red light he slipped the cassette into the rack on the center console. "All right, I think I'm comfortably numb enough. Time for a little Russian roulette."

He gazed at the cassettes of Russian composers in his Classical section, and randomly ran his finger over the names of Stravinsky, Rachmaninoff, Rimsky-Korsakov, Prokofiev, Shostakovich, Khachaturian, and finally stopping on Tchaikovsky. His eyes widened as he contemplated how prophetic the selection was. "Ah, great choice!" he said, as he thought: *Then again, you can't go wrong with any of these darn Russkies.*

Darn, not because Armand didn't like Russians, it was only the political and military thugs he loathed, who turned their nation into an aggressive and oppressive machine, intent on devouring other nations. Unfortunately the Cold War had been escalating. Just recently, in response to the USSR's invasion of Afghanistan last year, President Carter had imposed a grain embargo. However, some of Armand's friends in the FBI, where he used to work, had ominous feelings about Afghanistan and the Middle Eastern region in general.

Nevertheless, as the light turned green, Armand stepped on the accelerator and slipped in the cassette. The Bose speakers ignited as the deep brooding strains of Tchaikovsky's *Manfred Symphony* oozed out. As he passed the Russian Tea Room, he couldn't help but think how so many Americans only knew Tchaikovsky for his famous and fanciful ballets, never having the good fortune of hearing his vast output of stunning symphonic poems, symphonies, and concertos that overflowed with unbridled passion and innovation.

He passed Carnegie Hall and turned south on 7th Avenue, then east on 56th Street, where he pulled into the parking garage. Hank, the garage attendant, ran to the distinctive '37 yellow Cord and opened the door. "Good evening, Mr. Arnolfini. The usual?"

"Yes, Hank, keep my beautiful canary safe. I'll only be two hours or so."

As Armand exited the exotic car, Hank hopped in and carefully parked it right next to the front office in a special stall surrounded by stanchions with red velvet ropes.

Armand entered Carnegie Hall, handed in his guest pass, and found his seat in the orchestra section, third row from the stage. An usher walked past and handed him a Playbill, which Armand eagerly opened. It was the hundred and fortieth anniversary of Tchaikovsky's birth and the gala tonight not only was featuring a fine selection of his music, but was premiering a display of artifacts and paintings related to the great Russian composer.

With a cacophony of discordant sounds, the orchestra readied themselves as they warmed up. Center stage was the massive black Steinway that Horacio Juarez would soon be manipulating, whereby luring the audience into the mind and genius of Tchaikovsky via his *Piano Concerto No. 1.*

Walking on stage to a welcoming round of applause was Andre Lamont, who mounted the podium, took a bow, and turned toward his talented assemblage of musicians. Once silence was obtained and the lights dimmed, Andre glanced at Horacio, who nodded, thus signaling the green light to commence.

With a swipe of his hand, Andre's baton launched the concerto. The orchestra punched out its eight introductory blasts when the lush iconic melody took over and sang its majestic tune. Some thirty-five-minutes later, the masterpiece reached its conclusion, as the audience applauded. Soon they wriggled in their seats, stretched their legs and, of course, coughed—vehemently.

Armand rolled his eyes. He had always found it odd how people only seemed to cough when classical music was played or during intermissions. He often thought that if people coughed like that in restaurants there'd be federal health laws passed requiring all patrons to wear facemasks, as not to contaminate other people or their meals. So how was it, he thought, that they only coughed like Flu victims in performing arts centers?

Armand shifted irritably in his seat, hoping the coughing would not ruin the next piece, which happened to be the symphonic poem *Romeo and Juliet*. Quite inexplicably, as Andre Lamont raised his hands, the hacking and coughing miraculously stopped.

Armand smirked. So they can control their coughing!

Meanwhile, the astute conductor took advantage of the brief moment of silence, as he quickly launched the piece. The soft and mesmerizing opening—riddled with sad undertones—brilliantly foretold the violent clashes of familial conflict and heartache that was soon to come. Building into a crescendo, the music exploded, as the full orchestra pounded out its fury, then slowly subsided, as a soft, romantic melody emerged from the storm. Armand sighed and slouched in his seat, breathing in its charm and beauty, when suddenly he heard an annoying *pop!*

He sat upright as his head spun, trying to locate the direction of the irritating sound. He glanced at the middle-aged woman sitting to his right, who merely shrugged her shoulders, then turned to his left. The elderly man next to him seemed not to notice or even care about the bothersome sound.

But then there was another *pop!* And another!

Andre Lamont pivoted around, at first annoyed, but as the audience began standing up, nervous and confused, Lamont briskly waved his hands, thus silencing the orchestra.

Someone yelled from the rear, "There's been a shooting!"

As panic set in, people dashed toward the exits. Armand jumped up and plowed his way through the hysterical crowd. Making his way into the lobby, he noticed everyone filing out the front and side doors. He made an about-face and headed down the corridors to the rear of the building. He came upon the manager, Oliver Whittaker, who gazed at Armand with petrified eyes. Swallowing hard, Oliver tried to bury the sorrowful sight he had just witnessed to greet his friend. "Arnolfini! I'm glad you're here."

"What happened?"

Oliver turned and pointed to the dead body on the floor. "That's Michael, my stagehand. He tried to stop the thief, but, but now he…he's d-dead." As he replayed the horrific memory in his mind, Oliver filled with rage, as he spat, "The brutal t-thug first carved him up with a dagger, then, after cursing him out in German, shot him t-three times. Three times! He's an animal! An utter animal!"

Armand compassionately grasped Oliver's shoulder. "Calm down, take a breath." He then noticed the dagger on the floor. It was a Nazi SS dagger. Armand walked over and looked at it closely. "Hmm, it's the real deal," he said. He turned back toward Oliver. "What did the thief take, and where did he go?"

Oliver glanced at Armand, still dazed and numb, as he tried to collect his thoughts. "Uh, well, he s-stole a painting, Armand, our prized *Tchaikovsky Memorial*, no less. It's by Silvio Riccadella. Quite exquisite and expensive." He paused briefly as he glanced back at the corpse of his young employee, then continued, "Evidently the animal stuffed it into a valise, which had a small eagle emblem on it, and ran out the rear entrance." Oliver pointed with his shaking finger. "Over there!"

"Call nine-one-one," Armand said commandingly, "I'm going after him!"

As Armand dashed toward the rear exit, Oliver called out, "But he still has a gun! Let the police handle this."

"No time to lose!" Armand exclaimed as he exited.

Armand ran into the street and saw a 1976 tan Mercury Cougar XR 7 tearing out.

An old feeble man was sprawled out on the curb; his groceries splattered all around him. Angrily, he gazed up at Armand. "Who the hell was that moron? That crazy fellow knocked me over and just took off!"

Armand helped the old man to his feet. "Are you all right? I mean hurt in any way?"

"Just my pride, son. You expect a little respect when you get my age."

"Well, I'm glad you're not hurt, but I have to run." As Armand took off toward the parking garage, he heard the old man call out, "Run where?"

"After that moron!"

Armand pulled out his extra set of keys and dashed to his '37 Cord. As he hopped in, he yelled out to Hank, "I'll square away with you later!"

The hide-away headlights of the old classic flipped open, looking like a sleeping dragon that awakened, with eyes blazing, while the Firestones burned rubber and the car lunged into the street.

Armand chased the red taillights of the tan Cougar, weaving between cars as best he could. The Cougar sped up and made a mad dash for the Queensboro Bridge, speeding through the intersection and onto the ramp. Armand pushed the pedal to the floor and tried to follow, but the Cougar had caused a large Mack truck to collide into two cars, which now blocked the entrance ramp.

Armand applied the brakes and cut the wheel hard right, now heading south. His mind reeled: *If this old-time Nazi stole a painting, I'll bet ten to one he's heading back to the Fatherland.* His eyebrows lifted. *Of course, JFK Airport.*

Armand raced down to the Midtown Tunnel, then made a beeline to the airport. Armand's fingers dug into the steering wheel. *I hope to God I'm right,* he thought. At this point, Armand felt he had nothing to lose; the Cougar had escaped him.

He pulled into the airport and coasted into the Long Term parking lot. He came to a stop and shut off the engine and lights, which retracted back into the fenders. His eyes surveilled the airport but saw no sign of the killer/thief. His hands tapped the steering wheel, anxiously, as his mind sank into a pool of doubt. He gazed at his watch. It was 9:36 PM. As each second and minute ticked closer to failure, Armand's vengeful fingers dug deeper and deeper into the steering wheel.

His mind reeled: *You dirty bastard, you couldn't just punch the stagehand; no, you had to mutilate the poor kid and then shoot him. Three times!* Armand shook his head. *Are you just a crazy American Neo-Nazi or the real deal?*

Twelve minutes passed. Armand glanced at his Rolex and huffed, dejected. *I couldn't have beaten him here by twelve minutes. Damn it, my guess was...*

Armand's eyes widened!

Right!

Just then the 1976 tan Mercury Cougar turned into the

Long Term parking lot at the adjacent terminal. Armand slipped out of the Cord and ran feverishly toward the Cougar as it pulled into a stall. Armand's sprints and stamina from his days of playing professional soccer had evidently not waned, as he zeroed in on his target, who was wearing a brown, army-style jacket and was just now exiting his car. Armand threw the first punch, but soon fists were thrown and grunts echoed in the night air. The thug's mean gnarly face twisted as he reached for his pistol, but Armand, with lightning speed, head butt him while simultaneously clipping his ankle with an illegal soccer move that he reserved only for creeps, whereby causing the thug to fall flat on his back.

Armand adroitly snatched the pistol and pushed the barrel into his face. "Who the hell are you?"

As the thug squirmed, Armand pushed his knees deep into his biceps while his left hand clasped the killer's throat like a vice grip.

The man's lips twisted with animus as he replied in a deep, German accent, "You *will* regret this. I swear!"

"No, *you* will regret mutilating a young man in cold blood and stealing a valuable painting!"

"Go ahead, kill me! I will *not* talk!" the murderous thief growled.

Armand eased up on his stranglehold and stood up, still pointing the gun at the animal's face. "Get up! Give me the valise with the painting. And if you make any silly moves, I *will* kill you!"

The man snickered. "You Americans can't kill anybody. You have laws, stupid laws that protect guys like me."

Armand cocked the hammer back. "Well, you don't know *guys like Me!*"

The man uneasily rose up to his feet while his hand slipped into his pocket and retrieved something. What it was, Armand couldn't tell, especially in the dark parking lot, yet the thug slipped the item into his mouth and bit down hard. Before Armand could process what happened, the thug fell to the ground as foam oozed out of his mouth—the toxic cyanide poison suffocating everything in its path as it raced through his veins. The writhing was extremely brief, as four violent convulsions and a final guttural gasp signaled the end of his life.

Armand recoiled in shock. *What the hell is going on? Suicide?* He glanced around the dark parking lot. No one was in sight. Some eighty yards away, the hustle and bustle of taxis, buses, and cars picking up or dropping off travelers continued without a hiccup, while Armand's poor brain was blindsided by a flurry of hiccups. It was like his mind was a strobe light, blinking rapidly as flashes of different options bombarded his senses.

He reached down and opened the man's brown army jacket, then slipped out his wallet and flipped it open. His eyes squinted as he thumbed through the stack of West German Deutsche Marks, then widened as he slipped out a card that was hidden in a back compartment. It was old, yellowed and tattered. It was a Waffen SS card. It read Helmut Hein, SS-Untersturmführer.

Armand gazed down at the dead middle-aged man. He appeared to be no older than forty-five. Armand reached in and pulled out the dead man's passport and flipped it open. It read Helmut Hein. Armand huffed as he kicked the dead body. "What the hell were you trying to pull? You weren't old enough to be an SS officer."

He glanced around, realizing he spoke his thoughts out loud. *Shut up, Arnolfini! There must be a logical explanation.*

He searched through the wallet again, this time finding another card in the hidden compartment. It, too, was old and tattered, and read Helmut Hein II, Hitler Youth. *Ah ha! You sick little bastard. Like father, like programmed son.*

Armand then came across the dead man's airline ticket. Armand gazed at his watch. It was 9:55 PM and the flight was for 10:30 PM. Destination: Nuremberg, Germany. He tapped the documents against his hand, thinking. Suddenly he smiled, leaned down, and took off the dead man's army jacket and slipped it on. He gazed at the killer/thief's face, hair color, and body size, and despite the differences, figured he might be able to get past the airline clerk.

He didn't like disturbing a crime scene, but figured Helmut Hein might have been meeting his partner or an art collector at the Nuremberg Airport, so time was of the essence. He had to take the chance.

Armand retrieved the valise from the trunk of the Mercury Cougar and opened it up. There, inside, was the coveted painting by Silvio Riccadella, the *Tchaikovsky Memorial.* He couldn't help but admire the portrait of the famous Russian composer, which was embedded in a memorial featuring architectural aspects of St. Basil's cathedral and the Bolshoi Theater, with iconic symbols from Tchaikovsky's various ballets. He closed the case and straightened out his brown army jacket. He smirked, realizing it was a Hitler brown shirt replica, or more likely authentic. He made sure all his stolen documents and wallet were in order, then strolled into the Delta terminal and marched up to the check-in counter. With his head lowered, he handed his ticket and passport to the attendant, who fortunately was interrupted by her co-worker. The distracted attendant carried on her conversation, barely glancing at Armand's documentation, and processed his papers.

Armand turned quickly and began walking toward the gate when the attendant called out, "Excuse me, sir! I need to check-in your luggage."

Armand turned, and smiled. "No, thank you. It's a carry-on."

The attendant hadn't even noticed his appealing looks, but now smiled. "Have a nice flight," she said, as she turned back to her co-worker and giggled.

Armand sighed and kept walking.

Some fifteen hours later, Armand landed in Nuremberg at 7:30 PM. His hand was sweaty from holding the precious valise the entire flight, but as he deplaned and strolled into the terminal, his eyes intently surveilled the area. He walked slowly, hoping the art collector or partner would notice the valise with eagle insignia and approach him. What that person would say or do, Armand wasn't quite sure, but he knew the odds were great that someone there would recognize the prized valise or Helmut's Hitler-styled, brown-shirt army jacket.

He stopped to get a cup of coffee and a newspaper at the cafe and sat in the open lobby. With the valise under his arm, and the eagle emblem conspicuously displayed, he skimmed through the newspaper and sipped his coffee, as the fleeting minutes turned into two long hours. He groaned; he had waited long enough.

Armand pulled out Helmut's wallet and gleaned the home address on his driver's license, then hailed a taxi. As they drove through the quaint village of Nuremberg, with its narrow cobblestoned streets, Armand instructed the driver to pass the unassuming, yet now infamous, Kunstbunker.

The Art Bunker entrance was merely a set of two wooden doors with huge decorative hinges that was sandwiched between a line of apartments and shops on the village street of Obere Schmiedgasse. However, this vault was where the Nazi's had stashed precious works of art they had stolen during the war, along with historic artifacts from Germany, including works by Albrecht Dürer and the Royal Crown from the Holy Roman Empire. As they drove past, Armand surveilled the area, since he was well acquainted with the Art Bunker's notorious past. In fact, it was this Nazi hideout that solidified his hunch when he discovered Helmut's ticket to Nuremberg. As they drove on, Armand gazed up at the mountain behind the bunker, where he saw an impressive view of the old Imperial Nuremberg Castle. It was the spot where many had assumed the stolen art was stashed, but proved wrong.

The taxi finally arrived at Helmut's apartment, where Armand paid the cabby, pulled out Helmut's keys, and entered the flat. He placed the valise on the couch and opened it up once more to admire the prized painting. He was quite familiar with Riccadella's *Tchaikovsky Memorial,* as it had been reproduced on collector plates that retailed at performing arts centers in America and Europe. It was part of Riccadella's Pantheon of Composers collection, which featured several other great classical composers. Being a lover of the arts, Armand had collected several of Riccadella's plates himself, but there was nothing like looking at the original oil painting, with its vivid colors and intricate details.

Armand carefully shut the valise and leaned against it as he turned on the television. He gazed blindly at the TV screen, as his mind churned. *Why didn't someone approach me?* His baffled and weary mind conjured up a series of unanswered questions until his eyelids couldn't maintain the weight anymore, and he eventually nodded off, the jet lag taking hold.

The noises of the television changed from jovial commercial jingles to sappy sitcoms, then to serious news, when suddenly the door burst open! Before Armand could open his eyes, he felt a walloping thump and saw a bright flash of white light! The assailant had punched him square in the face. Instinctively, Armand raised his arms, and kicked hard! The assailant flew backward, landing on the floor. Yet as Armand regained his vision, he realized there were two thugs, as the other man, who was older, taller, and wearing a ten-thousand-dollar Kiton suit, reached for the valise. Armand grabbed the older man's wrist and twisted it inward, causing him to cave in by Armand's knees, whereby he wrapped his legs around the man's torso and pummeled him in the face, repeatedly, to a flurry of grunts and whimpers.

Meanwhile, the other assailant lunged at the entwined bodies and pried his older partner loose. Armand sprang to his feet, but the stocky young man pulled out a gun. "Move away from the valise, *mach schnell!*" he barked in broken English and German, as he wheezed from the earlier belly kick.

Armand took a step away from the couch.

Meanwhile, the older man pulled a handkerchief out from his classy suit and wiped the blood away from his split lips. He peered at Armand with his blue dagger eyes, as he slowly opened the valise. He gazed down at the painting, smiled, then shut the lid. He looked at his young cohort, *"Ja, es ist hier."*

Armand brazenly stepped toward the older man; while the thug with the gun stepped behind Armand, and barked, "Don't move!"

Armand faked a punch, then kicked the older man square in the chest. As he fell backward, Armand did the unexpected. He used a Pelé bicycle kick to clobber the thug behind him! Before the brute knew what happened, Armand had already been rotating upside down when his foot smashed him in the face. Armand's soccer stunt had changed the whole dynamics, as he bent over and retrieved the fallen revolver. As the two Germans wobbled to their feet, Armand pointed the pistol at them and said, "Okay, I enjoyed the tussle, but the game is over. Who the hell are you?"

Both men looked at one another, humiliated, then back at Armand. The older one, in the Kiton suit, snarled, "Never mind who we are, where is Helmut?"

The younger man, who was evidently the older man's henchman, remained silent.

Armand grasped the valise as he kept the gun aimed in their direction. "Your buddy, Helmut, is dead. Cyanide. Which tells me one thing, this operation of yours is extreme. And I'm talking about Nazi *fanatical* extreme."

The older man smiled condescendingly. "Nazis? Really? It is nineteen eighty. There are no Nazis left, you fool."

"I wish that were true, but Nazis are still being hunted down. Just a few years ago, Hermine Braunsteiner was found in Queens, New York. She was one of your evil, demented guards at Ravensbruck. She'll be going to prison, just like you two Nazi thieves."

Again the elderly man smiled and shook his head. "You have it all wrong. We are legitimate art dealers." He pointed to the valise. "And that painting, the *Tchaikovsky Memorial,* belongs to a Russian aristocrat. It was stolen from his collection and sold to the Carnegie Institute in New York. We're simply trying to return it to its rightful owner."

Armand sniggered. "Yes, you're art dealers, who just so happen to carry firearms, break into Carnegie Hall, kill an innocent employee, and now bust into my apartment. There are things called laws, gentlemen. And I'm not talking about anti-Semitic laws, like your infamous Nuremberg Laws of nineteen thirty-five, which were supposed to protect the purity of your rich Aryan blood. They also allowed Hermann Goering to start imprisoning wealthy Jews and art dealers to confiscate their valuable collections. And let's not forget, during the war Goering looted art museums in France, Belgium, Italy, and elsewhere, whereby amassing over twenty thousand pieces of artwork, some of which were buried in the Kunstbunker, right here in town." Armand gazed at them with reproachful eyes. "So I imagine you're just a bunch of leftover Nazis who still deal in stolen treasure; artwork that has never been recovered, or like this *Tchaikovsky Memorial*, that I'm betting you stole to sell to this rich Russian client of yours."

The two men glanced nervously at each other, as Armand added sternly, "So I intend to make sure you both suffer in prison for the rest of your rotten lives!"

With that, the young henchman tackled Armand onto the couch, where they both struggled, until the gun accidently went off. The Nazi thug let out an awful grunt as he rolled to the floor and held his bloodstained chest. His hands couldn't seal the breach as blood spurted out between his thick fingers, spraying the carpet and furniture like a lawn sprinkler. The fatal wound had struck his heart, which continued to pump the crimson liquid, as he gasped and trembled. Within several unnerving moments, he was dead.

Meanwhile, Armand had already stood up and once more pointed the gun at the distinguished elderly man in the suit. "I didn't intend that to happen, but if you try anything stupid, you'll end up just like him, a bloody mess. And I wouldn't want to ruin that expensive suit of yours."

The man's lips twisted in humiliation as he glanced down at his dead henchman, then back up at Armand. In his thick German accent he said, "You're an American, you have no jurisdiction here."

Armand waved the pistol. "*This* is my jurisdiction. But I happen to be Armand Arnolfini, a private investigator with strong ties to the FBI and Interpol, so either way, I *will* get what I want."

The man paused a moment, weighing his limited options. Then with a sigh, his once proud shoulders wilted. "My name is Herr Gerard Hoffmann. What exactly is it that you want?"

"I want the truth."

Gerard swallowed a lump of malice. "Well, you were partially correct, Mr. Arnolfini. Our Russian client is Boris Valdoff, a very wealthy man, with historic roots. He wants the *Tchaikovsky Memorial* for his personal collection, as he naturally has an affinity for all things Russian. But you were wrong about one thing. We are not Nazi remnants or art dealers, Mr. Arnolfini. We merely work for clients such as Boris, who deal in priceless stolen art and forgeries on the black market. He is the kingpin, the billionaire. His network is vast and would yield great returns for the art world if captured. Now the question I ask you is this: If I tell you where Valdoff is, will you let me go?"

"I think I can manage something, but you must personally take me to him, and—" Armand waved the pistol, "no funny stuff!"

"Agreed," Gerard replied. "He is in Stuttgart. It is only two and a half hours from here. We can take my car, if that's agreeable?"

"Sure, as long as it's not an Aston Martin with an ejector seat!"

Gerard cracked a halfhearted smile as he arrogantly shook his head. "You Americans and Brits are one crazy lot."

"Indeed we are, but not one millionth as crazy as you Super-*Stupid* Aryans."

Gerard's lame smile flipped into a scathing frown. "In that case, I'm rather disappointed. My car is only a Mercedes-Benz. No ejector seat."

"Okay, enough small talk, let's go!" Armand demanded.

Some two and a half hours later, they arrived at the Althoff Hotel in Stuttgart. Gerard Hoffmann had previously called Valdoff and arranged to meet at the hotel to make the exchange. Armand had instructed Gerard that he would pose as his new partner, Albrecht Schumann, and would have the pistol in his pocket, aimed at *him*, so no mishaps would be tolerated.

They now walked up the spiral set of stairs, and down the hall to room 256 to meet Valdoff. As they entered the suite, Boris greeted them with a welcoming grin, "Ah! Herr Hoffmann, so good to see you." Then peering at Armand, his jovial cheeks wilted with suspicion. "And you, I am told, are Herr Schumann, his new partner, *da?*"

"Yes, but please call me Albrecht. After all, we are all friends here. Right, comrade?"

Valdoff cracked a smile. "Naturally, comrade. Friends! Yes, friends!" he said as his lustful eyes glanced at the coveted valise in Armand's hand.

"Oh, yes," Armand said. "I'm sure you're very eager to see the *Tchaikovsky Memorial.*" He placed the valise on the table. "Allow me," he said as he opened the lid.

Valdoff stepped over and lifted the artwork up, gently, scrutinizing the brushstrokes, then extending it backward to admire the entire composition. "Magnificent! Truly brilliant," he said in his thick Russian accent. "We must celebrate!" he added, as he gently placed the artwork down. Then brutishly, he grasped a bottle of Stolichnaya Vodka, filled three glasses, and handed one to Gerard and another to Armand. *"Tebe!"* he cheered.

As they each returned a verbal salute and took a sip, Armand kept one finger on the trigger of the pistol in his pocket.

Evidently, Boris Valdoff had several vodkas before their arrival as he felt no pain, and for the benefit of Herr Schumann, he launched into a lengthy monolog about his family's royal roots and prestigious past. "I must tell you, Albrecht. I am a very important man. I am related to Catherine Pavlovna of Russia. Have you heard of her?"

Armand shook his head as he kept an eye on Gerard and took another small sip of vodka.

"Well, comrade, Catherine happens to be the Russian link, which married me, if you will, to my fellow Germans. You see, in the nineteenth century, Catherine had wed King William I of Württemberg. Württemberg, as you may know, includes this city. And it is here, in Stuttgart, where King William had the magnificent Württemberg Mausoleum built in her honor. Both monarchs are buried there." Boris staggered slightly as he walked to the window and drew back the curtain. "See, l-look there," he said with a slight slur. "On the mountaintop. Isn't it m-magnificent?"

Armand gazed out the window at the distant structure, which majestically mounted the peak. "Yes, it is marvelous."

Boris spun around to face his guests. "So, you see, Albrecht. It was my Russian family's connection to Germany, love of collecting and looting fine art, and my loathing of Stalin that made me partner up with Herr Hoffmann and—" Boris cut short his revealing tale upon seeing Gerard discreetly shake his head with piercing eyes.

Armand caught the exchange, stepped back two paces, and pulled the gun from his pocket. Valdoff's eyes widened as his ruddy face filled with rage. "You deceitful wretch!" he screamed as he unexpectedly charged Armand.

Armand smashed Boris in the face with the pistol, then quickly grabbed his neck with one hand and tripped him with his foot. Boris fell face-first, hitting his head on the corner of the end table and falling unconscious to the floor. Before Gerard could make a move, Armand cocked the revolver. "Don't even think about it! You see what happens when half-wits mess with me."

Gerard stood motionless and mute, as Armand felt Valdoff's neck for a pulse. "The drunken Cossack will be fine. But you *won't be* if you don't cooperate." Armand stood erect and queried sternly, "Where are you stashing all the stolen art? Is it back at Nuremberg?"

Gerard remained silent, as Armand added, "Or is it right here, in Stuttgart?"

As Gerard's face twitched, Armand smiled. "Of course it is." He turned and looked out the window. "In the beautiful Württemberg Mausoleum." Gazing back at Gerard, he demanded, "And you're going to take me there!"

He reached down and extracted Valdoff's keychain from his pocket. "I imagine one of these will do the trick. Unless of course, you have the key?"

"As I told you," Gerard finally spoke. "Boris is the kingpin. I have no idea where he stores his stockpile of art."

"Sure you don't. You're just an innocent pawn in this whole scheme. You must think I'm a chump," Armand blustered. "Your buddy Helmut had an SS dagger that he used to mutilate a young stagehand. He was also a brown shirt, a Hitler Youth fanatic, who even committed suicide, like your cowardly Führer. And my guess is that you were part of the Kunstshutz, the Art Protection squad that protected works of art. Or should I say, '*looted* works of art.'" On second thought, Armand added, "Or perhaps you worked directly for Goering, in his Rosenberg squad, which bypassed the Kuntstshutz to expand his personal collection."

Once again, Gerard remained stubbornly silent and stiff as steel.

Armand grasped the valise and pointed the gun at the Nazi's head. "Now move!"

Traveling in Gerard's Mercedes, they drove up the winding roads of the mountain and finally arrived at the peak. Standing before them was the impressive burial chamber. Built after the archetype of all domed buildings, namely the Pantheon in Rome, the Württemberg Mausoleum was a circular domed structure with three porticos and an entrance, which sat atop a flight of stairs decorated with four large urns mounted on pedestals.

Armand left the valise in the car's trunk and motioned to Gerard to walk in front of him. As they entered the majestic edifice, Armand was struck by the size of the mausoleum's interior, for it had previously been used as a Russian Orthodox Church up until 1899, and has remained in use to annually celebrate the Pentecost.

Armand spun his head around to look at the stunning, all-white interior, with its large coffered dome, adorned with rosettes, then down at the circular walls with columns, and finally landing on the iconostasis, decorated with oil paintings of various saints. "Very beautiful," Armand said. "But I doubt those six paintings account for the lucrative stash you have stored here." He turned toward Gerard. "So, where are they, Herr Hoffmann? Or do you prefer that I call you by your SS rank? After all, I wouldn't want to insult a high-ranking Nazi officer, now would I?"

Gerard's lips and slick eyebrows twisted with venom, not appreciating the sarcasm. "Yes, at this point, you might as well show me some respect, Mr. Arnolfini. I am SS-Gruppenführer Hoffmann. I was one of Goering's most trusted and efficient group leaders, and did indeed head his Rosenberg division. You are quite clever, Mr. Arnolfini. But for the record, the Kuntstshutz amassed more than twenty-*two* thousand works. We had works by Degas, Vermeer, Da Vinci, Raphael, Matisse, and many more!" He took out his white handkerchief and wiped the saliva from his heated lips, then added, "And yes, Boris was a buffoon! a spoiled, silver-spooned mediocrity who inherited massive wealth and never worked a day in his drunken, miserable life. He would have blown his entire family's fortune if not for me!"

"Very impressive, but I'm not impressed," Armand retorted as he aimed the gun at his head. "Now show me where you hid all the artwork."

True to form, the SS-Gruppenführer remained rigid as a rifle, arrogant as an Aryan, and stubborn as an SS-mule.

Armand smirked as he lowered the gun, while his eyes scanned the circular interior of the mausoleum. Then they gazed down at the large, wrought iron circular grating at the center of the brown, checkered-tiled floor. "Naturally," he said, "it must be in the crypt below. After all, your rabid mole, *Der Führer,* had a penchant for subterranean bunkers." Armand noticed the thick wooden door with a large padlock. He pointed the gun at Gerard, once again. "Let's go! That must be the entrance."

As they approached the large door, Armand pulled out Valdoff's keychain and inserted one key after another until it unlocked. He instructed Hoffmann to walk in front of him, down the dark steps into the crypt below. The curved-block walls and narrow stairs spiraled downward into an even darker and smaller stairwell that Armand was finding visually oppressive and unsettlingly claustrophobic. As they arrived at the lower level, light from the circular grating above shed a faint glow on the center of the floor, as well as on William and Catherine's tomb across the expanse. Armand looked around the circular chamber; he didn't see any paintings or doors. "Okay, Gruppenführer Hoffmann, where's the access panel?"

Again, Hoffmann remained militantly mute.

"My offer still stands, Gerard. If you help me, I'll do whatever I can to mitigate your case."

The Gruppenführer laughed disdainfully. "As you can see, Mr. Arnolfini, I am not a young man. And as they say, I was not born yesterday. You will not be able to mitigate my sentence, for as I told you; I am the mastermind of this operation, not Boris Valdoff. As such, Interpol and the German government will want my head."

Armand wanted to smash him *in the head,* but knew the loyal and obedient Nazi would never talk. His eyes scrutinized the dark interior of the crypt and spotted two statues, each in niches. One was of Moses and the other Mary Magdalene. Armand smiled as he stepped toward the statue of Mary, while still keeping his revolver aimed at Gerard's head. He noticed that the niche around the statue had an open seam. He grasped the statue with his free hand and pulled. As he anticipated, the entire niche with statue swiveled outward, revealing a steel door with a lock. Once again, he used Valdoff's keychain and managed to unlock the door.

Gerard nodded. "*Impressive.* Good guess, or perhaps just luck."

Armand smirked. "It wasn't luck, Gerard. No anti-Semitic Nazi would choose Moses. He freed the Jews. You morons cremated them."

"And thank God we did!" the Gruppenführer spat.

Armand smirked. "What did you Nazis know about *God*? Other than being his fallen angels."

Gerard hissed. "God himself used brimstone and fire to eradicate the wicked, Mr. Arnolfini! We knew well what had to be done."

"Yes, He did, but your brimstone and fire *backfired*, burning and razing Nazi Germany to a pile of rubble and dead carcasses. Many of your remaining leaders were round up and hung or committed suicide. It worked out *divinely.* Now, shut the hell up!" Armand flipped on the light switch, which illuminated a set of stairs that led into another chamber below the crypt. He pointed the gun at Gerard and instructed him to walk down first, as he followed. The damp musty air was oppressive and nauseating until they reached another steel door below. As they entered the chamber it was clear that the air temperature and humidity were precisely controlled. Armand's eyes widened in awe!

There before them, was a stash of over fifty works by various masters, such as Rembrandt, Rubens, Degas, Monet, Bouguereau, Gerome, Dou, Caspar David Friedrich, and among others, a Vermeer.

Armand walked slowly past the paintings, savoring each glorious vision. "Now, *this* is what I call *impressive*, Gerard." He eventually stopped at the Vermeer, glanced at the work, then gazed back at Gerard. "But this one is *not* so impressive."

Gruppenführer Hoffmann squinted. "What do you mean *not* impressive!? It's *Christ with the Woman Taken in Adultery* by *Vermeer*, perhaps one of the most valuable acquisitions Hermann Goering ever acquired."

Armand chuckled. "Gerard, I happen to be an aficionado of art, especially from the Renaissance to Baroque periods. And I also know the amusing history behind this particular piece."

Hoffmann's face radiated contempt. "What do you mean *amusing*?"

"I know very well that Hermann Goering traded one-hundred-and-fifty paintings he had looted, each by lesser-known artists, to acquire this Vermeer. But it's a fake! It's by forger Han van Meegeren. Your infamous fat man was duped!" Armand started laughing, while Gruppenführer Hoffmann gritted his teeth. "So, you know your art history very well, Mr. Arnolfini. But for your information, I was on the threshold of selling that fake for a sizable sum to an ignorant private collector. Namely, Boris Valdoff."

"Well, I'm sorry to ruin your lucrative racket, Gerard, but like your flamboyant master, Hermann Goering, it's time to head back to Nuremberg to stand trial for your sins." With that Armand pointed the pistol at his head. "Let's go, up the stairs!"

Gruppenführer Hoffmann's face radiated disgust as it turned crimson red. "I will *not* be humiliated by my *inferiors*!" he blasted. With a swift blur, Gerard pulled a cyanide capsule out of his pocket, popped it in his mouth and bit down hard! Before Armand could react, the toxic ion poison surged through Gerard's body, suffocating his heart, nerves, and muscle tissues, causing violent seizures, and ultimately, an agonizing death.

Armand stood bewildered and pensive. He shook his head, not understanding the fanatical nature that grips some people. Moreover, the fact that Nazi fugitives still remain, hidden in various corners of the world, was a disturbing thought. But he was glad to finally put this reprehensible art ring to rest once and for all. Hitler and Goering were the two biggest art thieves known to mankind, and despite ending this repugnant remnant of the Reich, Armand wondered how many masterpieces the Nazis had stolen or maliciously destroyed that would never see the light of day again.

After spending several hours explaining to the Stuttgart police and Interpol the roles of Gerard Hoffmann and Boris Valdoff, who had awoken from his concussion, Armand returned to Nuremberg, where he explained the death of Gerard's henchman to the police. He then spent several hours speaking to the hospitable villagers, content in knowing that the malignant Nazi virus had in large measure been eradicated, and that the honorable and industrious Germans of the day had made a miraculous comeback into the civilized world, becoming one of the wealthiest and innovative of nations. Offering many of those he met his deepest hopes that they would be reunited one day with their East German kin, he then took a taxi to the airport and returned home, landing at JFK Airport.

He walked across the street into the Long Term parking lot and started up his classic '37 Supercharged Cord, then drove straight to Carnegie Hall. There he met Oliver Whittaker, where he told him about the Russian link, namely, the convoluted tale of how the *Tchaikovsky Memorial* had led to a Russian/German Mausoleum in Stuttgart and eventually to an old Nazi art scheme. The *Tchaikovsky Memorial* was placed back on display, as millions came from all over the world to celebrate the anniversary of Tchaikovsky's birth with first-rate performances and a dazzling display of rare artifacts and, of course, Silvio Riccadella's stylish painting, which now had a history-making tale of intrigue added to its resplendent aura.

The P.T. Barnum Mystery

Armand Arnolfini's eyes widened with curiosity as he pulled up to *The Barnum Museum* in Bridgeport, Connecticut. The exotic beauty and nostalgic charm of the old brick and etched-stone museum appeared to be an apparition of grander days as it sat amid a bland, ultra-modern white building that intrusively encircled the historic edifice. Arnolfini frowned. He was well aware that architecture reflected the cultural and moral integrity of its time and, as far as he was concerned, the sophisticated craftsmanship and beauty of the nineteenth century far surpassed the square, flat, and vapid structures that populated the modern era. To Armand, it was clear: profits had trumped creativity...not to mention humanity.

He shifted his classic, '37 yellow Cord into neutral, came to a stop, and pulled the emergency brake. Armand sat for a moment, just gazing up at the enchanting

Byzantine/Gothic edifice in wonder, with its unique integration of styles and large inscription that ran across its curved façade: *The Barnum Institute of Science and History.*

Walking toward his dashing Cord, Andrea St. John, the museum's curator, eagerly approached him. "Armand, it's nice to finally meet you!"

She reached over and grasped the door handle as Armand simultaneously opened the door. Stepping onto the sidewalk, Armand closed and locked the door, while keeping his eyes on Andrea. She was much prettier than he expected. "Thank you for the invitation, Ms. St. John." He glanced up at the captivating façade of the building once again. "I had no idea this museum even existed, or that P.T. Barnum ever had it built."

Andrea's warm smile mellowed to a pout. "Yes, it's rather sad that most people have no idea about all of the things Phineas Taylor Barnum engaged in." She peered over her shoulder at the marvelous structure. "That's what this museum and my mission are all about. In fact, this building is the only one remaining of Mr. Barnum's, and there were many: from several mansions to his wildly popular museums and hippodromes."

She extended her arm toward the main entrance. "Allow me to show you some of our exhibits, which will enlighten you to the spectacular world and wonders of P.T. Barnum."

"By all means!" Armand replied, enthused.

As they entered the building, Andrea pointed to a large display panel with the words '*General Tom Thumb*' accompanied by a life-sized photo of the little man. "As you can see, we also feature Mr. Barnum's most popular attractions."

Armand glanced at the photo of Tom Thumb with interest as she went on, "Tom was actually related to P.T., and was only twenty-five inches tall at the peak of his teens."

Armand shook his head, as he glanced at her, then back at the photo. "Surely you jest? No dwarf could possibly be *that* small, could they?"

Andrea pointed to the two-foot ruler in the photo, which Tom stood next to and surpassed by only one inch. "Well, Charles Stratton—better known by his stage name, Tom Thumb—was indeed *that* small. However, after his teens, Tom did manage to grow to approximately forty inches tall. He, too, had become immensely famous in his day, even appearing before Queen Victoria and the Tsar of Russia."

"Yes, I'm aware that P.T. Barnum was the greatest advertising wizard in his day," Armand said, while he curiously surveilled the museum's displays. As he did, his eyes landed on a bizarre exhibit: the skeleton of a centaur. "Surely *that* never existed!"

Andrea followed his line of sight, then giggled. "Yes, Mr. Arnolfini, that never existed. But, as you can see, Mr. Barnum was the first American on record to realize humankind's strange fascination for bizarre curiosities. Long before he started his famous circus—which is sadly the only thing he's remembered for—Phineas served as a senator, and a mayor, while also being one of America's most innovative and successful entrepreneurs in his day. For example, he sparked an interest for opera in America by bringing Jenny Lind, known as the 'Swedish Nightingale,' on tour, which grossed three-quarters of a million dollars— an astronomical amount of money for that time. He also conceived, and had built, the *American Museum* in downtown Manhattan, which featured educational lectures, peculiar entertainments, and even introduced the first aquarium in America, which housed beluga whales in the basement. P.T. also built the *Great Roman Hippodrome*, which evolved into today's Madison Square Garden."

Armand shook his head, fascinated. "Gee, I'm sad to say, Ms. St. John, that I'm one of the many poor souls in the dark regarding Mr. Barnum." Armand peered around at all of the displays. "Evidently, the man was far more than a showman."

"Yes, he was," she agreed as she glanced at the nostalgic poster of The Barnum and Bailey Circus. "What most people also don't realize is that he only started his famous circus at the ripe old age of sixty-one."

Once again, Armand shook his head in amazement. "I never knew that. Actually, it's inspiring to know that it's never too late to be creative and productive." Just then, his eyes caught a glimpse of a bizarre sight—a fanciful illustration of a weird creature, apparently half-monkey and half-fish. Unable to draw his eyes back to the pretty curator, Armand stared at the monstrosity, attempting to make heads or tails of it, literally.

Andrea noticed his fascination. "Well, that *thing* is why I called you."

Still unable to take his eyes off the peculiar illustration, he was compelled to move closer to inspect the creepy image more thoroughly. As he did, he said, "This looks like something Hieronymus Bosch conjured up."

Andrea stepped up alongside him. Discreetly, she looked up at the tall and handsome P.I. with interest, then at the ugly image. "No, this isn't one of Bosch's weird concoctions. This creature was called the Feejee mermaid, Mr. Arnolfini."

Armand finally broke his stare and looked at her. He laughed. "Dear Lord, that's one ugly mermaid!" As Andrea also laughed, he added, "All the mermaids I've ever seen—

like Daryl Hannah in *Splash*—were all quite beautiful. Half-woman, half-fish."

"Yes," she said with a smile. "Daryl *did* make for an attractive mermaid, but that wouldn't be something Barnum would have cared to exploit. Unless, of course, she could sing like Jenny Lind."

As they both chuckled, Armand said, "Very true, Madison only shrieked."

Andrea then pointed to two old photographs, each depicting Barnum's *American Museum* that once stood in lower Manhattan. One showed the towering museum in all its glory, while the other was a disturbing image. It was the after-photo of when the museum was terribly burned and disfigured in the fire of 1868.

Armand looked at the photo, then solemnly at Andrea. "I hate seeing great works of ingenuity, architecture, or art destroyed. What happened?"

Andrea shrugged. "No one knows for sure. Gas lighting, or even the use of candlelight, were often the cause of fires before the advent of electricity. As you know, many important buildings and artifacts had been lost over time due to the dangers of open flames indoors." She peered back at the ugly illustration of the Feejee mermaid. "And that's why I summoned you, Mr. Arnolfini. I hear you're the best private investigator out there, especially since your forte is art-related crimes. Bernard Higley of the *Cloisters Museum* had told me much about you."

Armand nodded thoughtfully. "Ah, yes, good ol' Bernie. So *that's* how you got my name?"

"Yes," she said. "When I read about the Phantom Forger case in the *New York Times* a few years ago, I remembered it was connected to the *Cloisters Museum*. So, when I recently decided to start an investigation of my own, I called

Bernard. We knew each other back in college. And, well, he told me *you're* the man to do it."

Armand squinted. "Do *what*, exactly?"

She turned back toward the eerie illustration. "I'd like you to find the Feejee mermaid."

Armand glanced back at the creepy drawing and laughed. "Seriously? You even said so yourself, there's no such thing as that ugly creature. And thank God for *that*!"

Andrea chuckled. "Yes, of course there's no such thing as *that*, Mr. Arnolfini. But, P.T. Barnum had leased that alleged creature from a Mr. Moses Kimball to put it on display, which became a major sensation in its day. Barnum even had a Naturalist inspect the taxidermized creature, to see if it was real or a fake."

Armand stepped back and raised his hands, palms out. "Hold on! This is *way* out of my wheelhouse, I'm afraid."

Andrea crossed her arms. "So, that's it—you're afraid?"

Armand chuckled as he lowered his hands and head. His eyes rolled up, catching her clever smile, then reconnected with her alluring, sea-green eyes. He raised his head. "Okay, it's not that I'm afraid, Ms. St. John. It's just that mythological sea monsters are *not* my forte."

"Mr. Arnolfini, don't look at this as some silly sea-monster hunt. Of course we're all of the same mindset that this was just another hoax, a fabricated object meant to garner attention and ticket sales. But, nonetheless, it *was*—and perhaps still *is*—a historical artifact of great public interest and monetary value. This oddity, or stage prop, *did* exist, Mr. Arnolfini. But it was never seen again after the great fire of 1868, when the *American Museum* burnt down."

Glancing back at the drawing of the odd creature—with its monkey head and torso attached to a fish's body—Armand crossed his arms and nodded slightly, some three or four times. "Yes, yes, yes, I can see it now." He looked back up at her, steadily, seriously. "This *is* a fascinating piece of Americana. But, *where* do I even begin? The *American Museum* burnt down over a hundred and twenty years ago."

Andrea's eyebrows and lips twisted in thought. "Good question, Mr. Arnolfini. If I knew, I wouldn't have needed to call you. *You're* the detective."

"Yes, but even detective work requires good leads. And the only lead you offered has been burnt to a crisp, literally."

Andrea gazed into his vibrant brown eyes with a growing interest and a tad more than pure business on her mind. She hadn't expected Armand to be so handsome and charming, yet she wasn't about to ruin her professional decorum with any overt personal overtures. However, subtle seduction, she thought, was fair game, as she said, "That's why I called you, Armand. I know that *you*—the celebrated art aficionado-*slash*-P.I.—can figure it out, somehow."

Armand clearly noticed the tantalizing glitter in her eyes that accompanied her flattery, yet he wasn't sure if it was personal attraction or sly business acumen. "Very well, Ms. St. John. You've piqued my curiosity…and stroked my ego, quite effectively, may I add. So, I can easily see why you chose to be the curator of a museum that lauds the Greatest *Showman* on Earth."

Andrea smiled and extended her hand. "Believe me, it's not all showmanship, Armand. So, do we have a deal?"

He shook her delicate hand with a smile in return. "A deal it is, Andrea. Yet, like Mr. Barnum, we *will* have to talk money."

"Of course," she replied, with the smile of a clever businesswoman. "Come into my office."

With that, Armand and Andrea discussed the finances required, then sat down and reviewed various details about the artifact's history. Diligent as ever, Armand inquired about P.T. Barnum's life and any information that might be pertinent to the case. During that time, it became clear that each tried to conceal the attraction that exceeded their fascination with P.T. Barnum, as subtle smiles and gestures enlivened their meeting. Four hours later, Armand said goodbye in a purely businesslike fashion, then hopped in his flashy Cord and drove back to his Manhattan apartment on the Upper East Side.

As he sat at his exquisite Renaissance dining table, he scoured the archival documents and copies of P.T. Barnum's personal letters, which he obtained from Andrea. Two hours later, with his eyes tiring, he pushed the documents aside and grasped the dish he had prepared earlier. Neatly arranged on the plate were slices of prosciutto, fresh mozzarella, red peppers, and a variety of olives. As he picked at the antipasto, his eyes scanned the walls of his elegant apartment. His refined taste for Medieval, Renaissance, and Baroque artifacts and artwork, which included the modern ones he inherited from Paolo Santanello, not only satiated his weary eyes, but also uplifted his very heart and soul. As Arnolfini firmly believed, great art had a way of elevating the human spirit, for creativity was the magical catalyst that could inspire and urge others on, to think differently, and to expand one's horizons. And, in turn, keep the wheels of progress turning.

As he swallowed a salty piece of prosciutto, his eyes landed on his framed print of *The Coliseum* by Lawrence Alma-Tadema. Armand squinted.

Of course! he thought. *The Roman coliseum—the archetype that all arenas followed, just like Madison Square Garden.*

He grabbed his keys and dashed out the door. He drove down to midtown, where he entered the Garden's parking lot. He located a supervisor and managed to gain access to the basement and, in particular, to any old or abandoned storage facilities. Armand rummaged through all the known chambers, yet without success. Disappointed, Armand put a call in to his friend, Joe Boccia, at the New York City Department of Buildings. He asked Joe to pull out a set of the Garden's architectural drawings, dating back to its earlier incarnations. Joe's response was unexpected.

"Armand, you're at the wrong location."

"What do you mean?" Armand glanced around. "I'm *at* Madison Square Garden."

"Yeah, Arnolfini, but that's the *latest* location. It existed in not one, but *two* previous locations in Manhattan."

Armand's shoulders sank. "That's just swell. The curator of *The Barnum Museum* informed me that the Garden's lineage could be traced back to P.T. Barnum's *Great Roman Hippodrome*. Is that true?"

"That's the story, all right," Joe replied. "Barnum had built the *Hippodrome* as an open arena, where he featured Jumbo the Elephant and many other strange acts. However, his bad luck with museums, which had burnt down several times, led to his idea of designing an open–styled venue, like the Roman coliseum."

"So, where *was* Barnum's *Roman Hippodrome* located?"

"Downtown, where the old train sheds used to be in the late 1800s. Let me see… Oh yeah, at Madison Avenue, between 26th and 27th streets. Hence the name *Madison* Square Garden." He paused, then queried, "Just what is it you're searching for this time, Arnolfini? The bones of Jumbo?"

Armand chuckled. "No, not an elephant, Joe. The Feejee mermaid."

He could hear Joe laughing through the receiver, whom upon catching his breath, said, "A freakin' mermaid! Have you been drinking, Arnolfini? Or smoking weed?"

"You know I don't smoke, Joey, and I'm not drunk. The Feejee mermaid was some bizarre prop that Barnum put on display. It's got a monkey's head and upper torso with a fish's body and tail."

Joe laughed harder. "She sounds like a real beauty, Armand." Adding a touch of his typical ribald humor, he rattled on, "I know some kinky guys hook up with blow-up dolls, but Christ, a Feejee mermaid with a monkey's head... Dear Lord, are you *that* lonely?"

"Okay, Joey, I guess you've made a monkey out of me with your fishy *tail*," he wittily replied, "but seriously, this artifact could be worth millions, if I can locate it."

Joe's hysteria died instantly. All Armand could hear was silence, until Joe finally replied, "Ah, so I see. This really *could* be something big, huh?"

"Yes, Joey, it certainly could be. Listen, I have to run. But, thanks for your help."

"Sure, no problem, Arnolfini. Once you find this monkey-fish, maybe we can hook up for a drink...at the zoo. Or would it be the aquarium?"

Armand chuckled. "I'll certainly let you know, *if* I find this ugly hybrid. But it won't be easy, Joey. Certainly not as easy as shooting fish in a barrel...of monkeys."

Joey laughed. "Go on, get outta here! Happy hunting. I'll talk to ya soon."

With that, Armand hopped into his iconic Cord and traveled to the two previous sites of the Garden, then down to where Barnum's *Roman Hippodrome* once stood. He had searched through the basements of each of the current buildings and found nothing, not even a lead. His shoulders wilted as he walked down the street toward the parking garage. The whole day was shot searching buildings and basements for an artifact that, most assuredly, he thought, had been destroyed in the 1800s. Dejected, Armand slipped into his car, started it up, and flicked on the hideaway headlights, which rolled up out of the front fenders. With the sun setting and casting a golden hue across the façades of glass and steel buildings, Armand shifted into gear and headed uptown to his apartment.

Once at home, he strolled in and sat on his authentic Savonarola scissor chair. His weary mind wondered, *Where else could I possibly look for this crazy, monkey-mermaid? It had to have burned in the fire.* He gazed down at the historic chair he was sitting in. The coincidence was jarring. *Jesus! It burned, just like Savonarola had burned.* He stood up and shook his head. *What the hell am I doing? This infernal quest is useless.*

Once again, he sat at his precious dining table, carved in 1478. Its four legs were shaped like those of a lion, which tapered down into the claw of an eagle grasping a ball. Armand slumped over the documents and letters and stared aimlessly at the wall. Burning thoughts of Savonarola's bonfire of the vanities clouded his mind, as well as visions of the Dominican friar being led to the gallows for heresy and being burned.

Armand himself felt burned out, as his head fell into his hands. With his eyes closed, Armand took a deep breath and exhaled with a sigh. In the blackness of his mind, he searched for a clue: a spark of something, anything. But all he could see was a black void. No clues, no ideas. *Nothing.* He opened his eyes, only to see the copies of Barnum's extant letters scattered on the table. Then, there it was; a prominent name glared out of the page, one that aptly lit his mind up like a light bulb: Thomas Edison!

Armand moved his elbow to gain a full view of the letter that Barnum had written to his electrical-wizard friend. Excited, he read it to himself, out loud.

"Dear Thomas, my luminous friend, I hear you will be staying at *The Cliff House Hotel* near Pikes Peak in Manitou Springs. I wish to join you there, not only to take in the beauty of the Rockies and Mother Nature, but also to show you an unnatural oddity that Mother Earth bequeathed to us—namely, the mystifying Feejee mermaid."

Armand sat upright as a surge of adrenaline rushed through his body. He squinted. *Colorado? Edison and Barnum stayed at a hotel…in the barren wilderness of Colorado?*

He promptly dialed Delta Airlines and ordered a ticket for the following morning. Invigorated, he strolled into the kitchen, fired up the stove, and sautéed oil, butter, and garlic in one pan, and threw on a pot of water to boil his linguine. He opened a can of clams, added it to the simmering oil with fresh basil and parsley, and then opened a bottle of *Vernaccia di San Gimignano* white wine. A half hour later, after dinner, Armand capped off the night with a cup of cappuccino and a slice of his favorite dessert—tiramisu.

The next day, Armand landed in Denver, Colorado, and drove two hours south to Manitou Springs. As he pulled up to the historic hotel, he was taken aback. To see such an elegant building amid a rustic landscape made for an odd juxtaposition, yet one he found rather intriguing.

Why, he thought, would visitors to the wilderness desire such opulent accommodations? Wouldn't a log cabin have been more befitting?

Armand drove up the circular driveway and parked by the large front porch. He entered the hotel and, once again, was impressed by the beautiful Victorian architecture. He asked the clerk at the front desk to see the manager who, a moment later, entered the lobby.

"Hello, my name is John Mason. Welcome to *The Cliff House*. How can I help you?"

"How do you do, Mr. Mason. I'm Armand Arnolfini, a private investigator. And I—"

"Oh dear," the manager interrupted, concern marring his face. "Has there been a crime committed?"

Armand smiled. "Oh, no! Not at all. You see, I was hired by the curator of *The Barnum Museum* in Connecticut to locate a missing artifact."

The manager sighed with relief. "Oh, I see. And why would that item be here?"

"Well, I've had access to P.T. Barnum's private letters, and know that he stayed here. Actually, so, too, did Thomas Edison, who happened to room here at the same time."

The manager smiled. "Mr. Arnolfini, this hotel proudly boasts a stellar list of famous guests. We've hosted such luminaries as Teddy Roosevelt, Henry Ford, J. Paul Getty, Austrian Crown Prince Ferdinand, General John Pershing, Charles Dickens, F.W. Woolworth, Buffalo Bill, Jenny Lind, P.T. Barnum, and several others throughout our history."

Armand stood momentarily mute upon hearing the startling guest list. He peered around at the lush Victorian décor more closely. Returning his gaze to the manager, he said, "Very impressive. But, I'm still a little baffled as to why rich and famous people would travel all the way out here, in the wilderness, rather than Paris or Monaco?"

Mason nodded. "I suppose many people feel the same way, Mr. Arnolfini. But, you see, this hotel was actually built in 1873, before Colorado even became a state. Its first incarnation was simply a Western-style inn, which catered to hunters and trappers. Naturally, the beauty of Pikes Peak nearby was also a scenic draw. However, many years later, it was the mineral springs in the region that drew the wealthy, as they sought the water's mysterious healing powers."

"I see," Armand said, as he glanced at a decorative bronze statue of a woman, which was mounted on the newel post of the Victorian staircase. His eyes intuitively peered up the stairwell, then back at Mason. "Would you mind showing me to the room Mr. Barnum stayed in?"

"It would be my pleasure. Follow me."

With that, John Mason walked up several flights of stairs, down a hallway, and opened the door to the celebrity suite. As they entered, he said. "Well, Mr. Arnolfini, *this* is the P.T. Barnum suite." As they advanced through, he added, "But, I don't see how you could possibly find anything here that belonged to Mr. Barnum. Not only was his visit a century ago, but all of our celebrity suites have been completely renovated. We always keep the original look of the time period, yet update it with the latest amenities."

"I can see that," Armand said, impressed by the historical fidelity of the décor, as well as the high quality of the new Victorian-style bath fixtures. His shoulders slumped. It was painfully clear to him that the hotel's renovations surely eliminated any chance of finding the famous artifact, or *any* artifact left behind by one of its eminent guests. He scanned the room and sighed. He looked back at the manager. "Is there any chance I could see your attic and basement?"

Mason squinted. "What for?"

"Is it possible that items left behind by guests were stored in either location?"

The manager nodded slowly. "Actually, yes. There are a few things in storage, yet nothing—to my recollection—from that time period. Furthermore, the items we have are primarily small, and are of little to no value." He paused, then added, "Come to think of it, what exactly *are* you looking for?"

"I hate to say it," Armand said with a smile, "but, I'm looking for something called the Feejee mermaid. It's part mon...ah, never mind. Let's just say it's an oddity."

Mason chuckled and shook his head. "That's P.T. Barnum for you. Master Showman of the bizarre." He scratched his head. "Well, I can guarantee you, we don't have any mermaids in our attic or basement, Mr. Arnolfini. Odd or otherwise. But I'll gladly escort you there."

The two men climbed up into the hotel's massive attic and Armand searched through the piles of boxes, in nooks in the rafters, as well as in the tight corners of the hotel's small dormers. With no luck there, they both walked down five flights of stairs and entered the basement. Given free rein to explore once again, Armand searched every box, every bag, every item, and every hidden compartment. Yet, there was no Feejee mermaid to be found.

Armand looked at Mason, his whole demeanor wilting in defeat. "I'm sorry to have bothered you. I should have known this would be a wild goose chase."

"Well, I wish you luck on your quest, Mr. Arnolfini. But to alleviate some of your disappointment, I'd be glad to offer you a celebrity suite, as my guest."

Armand's frown rose to a weak smile. "That's very kind, Mr. Mason. But truly not necessary."

"Don't be silly, you need a place to stay, so please, take the room. Unfortunately, the P.T. Barnum suite is booked for this evening, but the Firestone suite is available."

"Thank you," Armand replied. As they began walking up toward the suite, he added, "Mr. Mason, you said 'Firestone suite.' As in, Firestone Tires?"

Mason looked back at him as they entered the room. "Yes, Harvey Firestone—tire and rubber manufacturing magnate. And good friend of Henry Ford and Thomas Edison."

"Of course, Thomas Edison."

"Why, of course?"

Armand shrugged. "Well, it was Barnum's letter to Edison that brought me here in the first place. And further along in that letter, Barnum mentioned wanting to meet up with Firestone, as well. What can I say, I just find it fascinating how all these titans crossed paths."

Mason patted Armand on the back. "Well, you've come to the right place for historical trivia like that, Mr. Arnolfini. I hope you'll enjoy your stay?"

Armand glanced around the unique, circular room and shook Mason's hand. "Indeed, I will, Mr. Mason. Thank you once again for your hospitality."

"My pleasure," Mason said as he turned and exited the suite.

Armand closed the door, walked over to the bed, and plopped down. He stared up at the domed ceiling and sighed. Gazing at the blank ceiling only reminded him of the dead end he had hit; worse yet, after having traveled thousands of miles to a remote hotel nestled in the Colorado Rockies it was now clear: his chances of ever finding the Feejee mermaid were just as remote.

Why the heck did I take on this case? he chided himself. *I told Andrea, right from the start, this wasn't in my wheelhouse.* He shook his head, knowing he should have followed his gut instincts.

Armand closed his eyes and soon fell into a deep sleep.

The vintage pendulum clock on the wall steadily swayed and ticked for an hour before Armand's eyelids started to part slowly. At first, his vision was a blur, but soon came sharply into focus, once again, on the domed ceiling. Only this time, the clarity was compelling!

Armand sprung out of bed, his eyes wide, as he gazed up at the circular ceiling.

Of course! This room is in the turret of the building. It has its own separate attic.

Armand picked up the telephone and dialed the front desk. Once the clerk answered, he said, "This is Mr. Arnolfini, in the Firestone suite. I wish to speak to your manager, John Mason, immediately!"

Fifteen minutes later, Mason knocked on the door, and was greeted by Armand, who had been busy thumbing through a large stack of Barnum's letters. Excitedly, he pointed up at the ceiling. "Is there an access panel to this turret's attic?"

Mason shook his head. "I'm sorry, but no. If there had been a hatch at one time, it was covered up with this decorative, domed ceiling."

Armand tossed the stack of letters, except for one, on the bed and anxiously ran his fingers through his thick, black hair with his free hand. "I have a strong, gut-feeling about this, Mr. Mason. You see, I looked through Mr. Barnum's original letters. In one, he states that he wished to show the odd mermaid to Harvey Firestone, who expressed an interest in the creature. So, I'm thinking that Firestone may have stored it in this room's attic for safekeeping, being that it's separate from the hotel's central attic, which anyone could access." Armand glanced up at the ceiling. "This turret's attic would have been the ideal vault, so to speak, for safeguarding a valuable artifact, which the Feejee mermaid most certainly was in its day."

Mason rubbed his chin. "But why would he leave it up there? Or Mr. Barnum forget it?"

Armand held up the letter he kept in his hand. "Well, while waiting for you, I uncovered another letter, which lends credibility to my hypothesis. This particular letter was written *after* their stay here, in which Barnum wrote to Edison, stating, 'If you see Harvey, tell him I want my mermaid.'"

Mason pondered Armand's words, and then nodded. "As crazy as all this seems, Mr. Arnolfini, there is an ample amount of logic in your proposition." He glanced up at the exquisitely finished, domed ceiling. With some reservation, he added, "I can't believe I'm even considering this, but I trust your judgment. For I, too, had a gut feeling, Mr. Arnolfini, one about *you*. I took the liberty of doing a little research on you, and came across quite a few articles about your famous investigations and international successes. Most impressive."

Armand appreciated the kudos, but right now, all he cared about was ripping open that beautiful ceiling to see what exactly was up there. "Thank you, Mr. Mason. So, does that mean we can open up this ceiling?"

"Yes. If you're willing to pay for the repairs."

"Most surely!" he said, as he gathered the letters on the bed and neatly placed them on the dresser. He looked at Mason. "To expedite this, let me say that I have experience using tools, Mr. Mason, and can make a small and precise opening, which your carpenter can close up and repair at your convenience. I would just need a keyhole saw, if you have one?"

"That would be acceptable, Mr. Arnolfini, as my carpenter happens to be on vacation, anyhow." Mason pivoted to exit, then stopped. "I'll get you the saw from our tool shed, and a drop cloth. We *must* keep this suite as pristine as possible."

"By all means!" Armand said as he began tidying up the room.

Twenty minutes later, Armand had placed the drop cloth down and stood on a ladder as he cut into the fine finish of the domed ceiling. After having cut out a small, square opening, he pulled out his penlight from his breast pocket and stuck his head up into the attic. As he swiveled around and shined the light upon the turret's rafters, the beam suddenly landed on an antiquated steamer trunk. Adrenaline rushed through Armand's veins as his eyes fixated on the old trunk. It was covered in dust and cobwebs, with the letters *"P.T.B."* stenciled on it. Armand's heart raced, as he eagerly pushed his way up into the attic and climbed toward the trunk. A large, iron padlock with rusted rivets—looking like one Harry Houdini might have used—firmly clamped the trunk closed.

The anticipation was unbearable. Swiftly, he passed the trunk down to Mason, and asked him to fetch a bolt cutter. No sooner did Mason return than Armand eagerly grasped the cutter and hacked off the old padlock. Kneeling before the trunk, the moment of truth was now upon him as he peered up at Mason, who winked. "Well, go ahead, Mr. Arnolfini. This is what you've been waiting for."

With that, Mason crossed his fingers as Armand turned back and slowly opened the lid.

Their eyes widened, as Armand gasped. Not only was the long-lost artifact in the trunk, but the hideous creature was so repulsive that Mason shivered, and blurted, "Dear God! Is *that* the monstrosity you've been searching for?"

Armand's stomach did somersaults as he squinted and inspected the bizarre creature closer. "Yes, I'm afraid so. I told you it was *odd*."

"Odd? That grotesque animal is downright repulsive. Did that thing really exist?"

Armand covered his nose. "Well, the story is that Barnum called in a Naturalist to inspect this aberration. Even *he* couldn't tell if it was a hoax—pieced together by some crazy prankster—or a genuine, genetic mutation."

Gingerly, Armand ran his fingers across the transition point, where the furry monkey's torso blended into the stiff scales of the fish's lower body. As far as Armand could tell, the joining was gradual and apparently seamless. Yet, he couldn't bring himself to believe such a creature could possibly exist. "I suspect that a very talented Taxidermist crafted this monstrosity." He looked back up at Mason. "We must remember; Darwin's Theory of Evolution was *the* most astonishing discovery of their age. The premise that mammals evolved from aquatic creatures, and mankind from *Homo habilis* almost three million years ago, spurred the imaginations of billions of people, including those with crazy notions, who wished to create tangible examples of Darwin's disturbing theory."

"*Disturbing* is an understatement!" Mason said, as he covered his mouth and gagged.

Armand pulled a handkerchief out of his pocket to cover his nose. "Indeed, it doesn't smell very pleasant, either."

Mason nodded heartily in agreement. "That's for damned sure! It's a nasty combination of dead fish and monkey ass!"

Armand laughed. He hadn't expected the refined manager to let his hair down. "Well, this monster has been stored in an attic for over a century, Mr. Mason. It's a good thing it was sealed in a trunk and that this ceiling was practically air-tight."

"Indeed," Mason said. "Otherwise, the guests in our Firestone suite would have upbraided us about the mysterious stench, thinking it to be vulcanized rubber!"

Armand chuckled as he stood up. "That reminds me—how much do I owe you to close up and patch this ceiling?"

"Never mind that," Mason said, as he wrapped his arm around Armand's shoulders. "All I want now is to take some photos of this historic moment, so we can add another fascinating tale to our storied past." He looked into Armand's eyes with deep appreciation and with the warmth of a new friend. "I'm honored to know you, Armand, and to have witnessed this epic moment."

"Thank you, John. And I'm glad to have found this relic in a historic site like *The Cliff House Hotel*."

With that, photos were taken, and the two men bonded further as their conversation drifted into a variety of topics. Later that evening, Arnolfini and Mason enjoyed a superb dinner in the hotel's elegant dinning room, then bid each other farewell.

Arriving at *The Barnum Museum* in Connecticut, Armand entered the building with the coveted trunk, as Andrea St. John ran to greet him. Overjoyed, she rose up on her tiptoes and kissed Armand on the cheek. "Thank you! Thank you! Thank you!" she exclaimed. She gazed down at the antiquated steamer trunk. "Well? Let's go! Open it!"

Armand smiled. "Okay, but cover your nose, it could use some Lysol."

As he opened the trunk, Andrea's eyes widened with delight. "Oh, my God! It's magnificent!" Covering her nose, she once again rose up and kissed Armand, this time with a warm embrace. "You have no idea how happy I am. Happy you found this relic, and happy that I hired *you*! You've lived up to your legendary status, Mr. Arnolfini."

Armand actually blushed, not only for the generous compliment, but also to be kissed by such a pretty and intelligent woman. A tingling sensation swept through his body as his face blushed deeper still. "Well, thank you, Ms. St. John. That's greatly appreciated."

Feejee Mermaid

Just then, a conservator approached, picked up the prized monkey-mermaid, and eagerly carried it away to start restoration.

Meanwhile, Andrea gazed into Armand's alluring brown eyes, as a feeling of regret came over her. "So, I guess this is it for us...you'll want your well-deserved check now, and will be on your way?"

Armand glanced at the floor as his mind jumped the rails, drifting from the tedious grind of work to the tender realm of emotions. "Actually, I'll take the check, Andrea, but I'd also like to take *you* out to dinner. Tonight, if that's acceptable?"

Andrea's heart fluttered as she struggled to restrain herself. She didn't want to be too assertive—a subtle smile would suffice. "T-that would b-be nice," she stuttered clumsily. She rolled her eyes and tried to recover. "I reckon dinner is to celebrate your historic find, Mr. Arnolfini. Correct?"

"Not exactly," Armand said, as his eyes peered deep into her sea-green orbs, which he keenly noticed had twitched with nervous anticipation. "We could certainly make a toast to the Feejee mermaid, Andrea, but this would be more of a...a *date*."

Andrea grinned in relief. "That would be nice, Armand. I know plenty of fine restaurants in the area. Is there anything in particular you like?"

Armand glanced at the illustration of the Feejee mermaid and smiled. "Well, we could do surf and turf." As she laughed, he grasped her hand. "And no worries, there won't be any monkey business!"

With matching grins, they walked out into the evening air toward Armand's dashing yellow Cord, then slid onto its plush leather seats. As its hideaway headlights rolled up out of the fenders, Armand shifted the car into gear. As they cruised toward *Sal's Steak & Seafood Grill*, the last golden rays of the sun cascaded across the ornate façade of *The Barnum Museum*, then faded slowly into an ethereal night, one teaming with expectations.

The Mark Twain Mystery

Outside, a cold winter breeze swept across the snow-blanketed streets of Bridgeport, Connecticut, while inside Andrea St. John's apartment, the warmth of a romantic fire crackled on the stone hearth. Softly playing in the background was the silky-smooth music of Barry White.

Armand Arnolfini gazed deeply into Andrea's lovely eyes as they clinked their flutes of champagne together. Andrea had gone all out on a bottle of Veuve Clicquot Brut Rose. Before them was a resplendent table she had set with two lit candles and two plates of filet mignon with garlic mashed potatoes on the side.

Andrea licked her moist lips. "Here's to our six-month anniversary," she said as she took another sip.

Armand smiled. "I can't believe how time flies the older you get. But I've really enjoyed these past six months, Andrea."

"So have I," she uttered with affection. She squinted.

"I've been meaning to ask...have you...dated other women since... Well, I mean since Cynthia passed?"

Armand's pleasant smile withered. "No. Actually, you're the first."

Andrea restrained a smile; happy to know *she* broke the ice. "How long has it been since she passed?"

Armand was reluctant to say, but answered: "Six years." He shrugged. "What can I say, some people call me a silly romantic. Others, a stupid fool...for closing the door on my personal life and getting lost in my work."

"Well, six years *is* a long time, Armand." Andrea hesitated, then said, "She must have been very special."

Armand nodded thoughtfully, solemnly. "Indeed, she was. I never really talk much about Cynthia...it hurt so much for so long. But I guess I can open up with you." He placed his flute down and paused a moment, then said, "Another reason why I abstained from dating was because of a silly pact she and I had made. In the swirling infatuation of youth, we swore to each other that if one of us died, the other would never fall in love again."

Andrea's heart dropped. "And you never did?" she murmured, as disappointment strangled her words.

Ever so slightly, Armand shook his head as his shoulders wilted. "No," he uttered, as his eyes solemnly rolled down toward his plate. He picked up his fork and tepidly poked his filet, as if it were sleeping.

The silence that followed was like a shish kabob skewer to Andrea's heart, as she bit her lip to contain the hurt. She now felt stupid for inviting him over for this silly six-month anniversary celebration, something younger couples did—certainly not those in their late thirties.

Armand's eyes rose, catching hers. "Well, until I met *you*, that is."

Andrea's face beamed as her heart jettisoned the skewer and fluttered with emotion. "You mean...*I* made you break your promise?"

Armand shrugged. "I'm afraid so."

She reached over and grasped his hand. "I feel—I don't know... I feel terrible, yet elated. I don't know what to say."

Armand smiled. "You've just said it. It's a bittersweet moment for me, as well, Andrea. Yet, I suppose it was inevitable that life would eventually take its course, regardless of the whims of two young lovers. All I can say now is, thank you! Thank you for breaking the long dormant spell that cloistered my heart for six years." Again, Armand picked up his flute and clinked her glass. "So, here's to us, and a brighter future."

Just as she was about to sip her champagne, her cell phone rang. She rolled her eyes as she reached over and grabbed her phone off the adjacent hutch. She was just going to turn off the ringer, but glimpsed the caller ID. She squinted, then gazed up at Armand. "It's Mary Havenshire, curator of the *Mark Twain House and Museum*. It must be important if she's calling me on a Saturday."

Armand placed his flute down. "Well, then answer it."

"But it's our anniversary, and a very special one at that."

"Don't be silly. Answer it. What we know in our hearts trumps all else."

Again, Andrea's face beamed as she answered the phone, while Armand finally sliced into his filet and took a bite. Yet as he gazed back up, Armand noticed Andrea's eyes widen as she said, "Okay, Mary, we'll be right there!"

Armand placed his fork down. "*We'll* be right there? What's going on?"

"Mary knows that we've been dating, and also knows that you're a private eye."

Armand chuckled. "Isn't *that* fascinating. And?"

Andrea stood up and placed a cover over her plate. "And she knows you're the best, silly. There's been a theft at the museum."

As she covered his plate, Armand slid his chair backward and wiped his mouth with Andrea's fancy silk napkin. "What was stolen?"

"She didn't say, but let's get a move on!"

With that the couple trudged through the snow and slid into Armand's classy '37 yellow Cord. As the antique plowed through the slush, she said worriedly, "I know you love this old classic, but I hope we don't get stuck in the snow."

Armand shifted gears. "Don't worry, this old beauty has front-wheel drive."

Andrea squinted. "You're kidding, only new cars have front-wheel drive."

"Not so," he replied. "Actually, the Cord auto company pioneered front-wheel drive back in the late 1920s. Unfortunately the Depression tanked the company, and the technology was forgotten for many decades. So this classic is truly *classic!*"

As Andrea smiled and nodded thoughtfully, Armand hopped onto I-91 North and, an hour later, they arrived at the *Mark Twain House and Museum* in Hartford, Connecticut.

As Andrea and Armand walked up the long flight of stairs to the museum building's main entrance, they came upon six policemen. One stuck out his hand. "Halt! The museum is closed until further notice."

Before Andrea could explain, Mary Havenshire walked into the vestibule and opened the glass door, as a cold breeze pelted her body and entered the building. "That's okay, officer, I called them. This is Andrea, curator of the *Barnum Museum*, and this is Armand Arnolfini, he is—"

"Ah! Mr. Arnolfini," the officer cut in, with an air of sarcasm. "The *great* art-crime detective."

As Armand's lips curled up into a smirk, the officer continued, "We don't need your *expertise*, Mr. Arnolfini. We've already apprehended the suspect."

Mary nodded as she continued to hold the door open "Yes," she said with a shiver, as she uncomfortably glanced at Armand. "I hate to say so, but over the past hour, much has happened. They found the thief and also reviewed the surveillance videotapes. They have him in custody. I'm sorry to inconvenience you both, especially on such a cold, wintery day."

"No problem, Mary," Andrea said as she rubbed her mittens together. "I'm just glad you found him."

A frigid wind blew across all of their faces, while Andrea pulled her coat's collar closer together. She was about to turn, when Armand clutched her elbow and started to walk her into the vestibule. "Excuse me," he said. "If you don't mind, we'd like to get out of this cold weather and warm up a bit before heading home."

As the officer heatedly looked at Mary, she shrugged and stepped aside as Armand and Andrea walked in. The policeman irritably followed, while Mary closed the door securely after him.

"Just out of curiosity," Armand said, looking at Mary, "can I see the video footage and the culprit?"

Mary uncomfortably glanced at the policeman. "I suppose it wouldn't hurt, Officer Portman. You've already solved the case."

Portman rolled his eyes. "This is totally unnecessary," he huffed. "But fine, have it your way." His heated eyes veered toward Armand. "Follow me."

As all four arrived in the security office, the museum's security guard dutifully rewound the video and hit play. On the screen, a view of Mark Twain's bedroom came into view. The room was empty for quite some time, until a disheveled young man with a scruffy beard and mustache, wearing a shabby gray hoodie, walked into the room. His face was clearly caught on film, but then the video flickered, and static filled the screen.

Armand rubbed his chin. "Why did it cut out like that?"

The museum security guard glanced out the window. "Because of the bad weather. We had lost power for a few minutes, but it came back on, as you'll soon see."

Sure enough, the video did resume, only to display Twain's vacant bedroom once again.

"Interesting," Armand said. "Very interesting."

Officer Portman pushed his way past Andrea, and retorted, "*What*? What is so *interesting*, Mr. Arnolfini? Winter storms wreak havoc on electrical lines all the time. You saw the young man enter the room, right? You saw his face—as clear as day—right? So, enough of this nonsense. You're wasting my time. We have the thief in custody, waiting to be booked."

"So, he's still here?" Armand inquired.

"Yeah, he's here, and I'm heading out, *right now*, to drive him downtown. So, this is where this ends, Inspector Clouseau."

"You can save your ornery remarks for someone else, Officer Portman. I'm not trying to step on your toes, but I must ask—how can you be sure you have the right man when the video cut out? We did not see him take the artifact in question, so you have no hard evidence. What you have is only circumstantial. It's pure suspicion."

"Mr. Arnolfini," Portman retorted, "when you see a wolf strut into a hen house, and the hens are found missing, the logical answer is that the wolf did it."

"Logic can only be accurate if *all* the facts are present, Officer Portman. But they're not. That missing segment of video clearly offers reasonable doubt. Logically speaking, of course."

Portman's lips twisted with contempt. "There's no need for me to tell you *anything* about this case, Arnolfini. But the fact is, we caught the guy, with the jewelry box in his hands, a few blocks from here."

"Okay, and what about the jewelry?" Armand asked. "Was that still in the box?"

Portman huffed as the veins in his neck began to bulge. "No. That's still missing."

"Ah, so I see. This case is *not* solved after all." Armand looked at Mary Havenshire. "I really would like the opportunity to speak to the suspect."

Mary sheepishly looked at officer Portman. "Well, he has a point, the most valuable items *are* still missing. Perhaps I might have to hire him after all. Please let him see the man in question, Officer Portman."

Andrea looked at Armand and winked.

A minute later, the young man was ushered into the security room in handcuffs by two officers. Armand's face instantly radiated doubt mixed with sympathy as he scanned the ragged young man before him: his missing teeth, odd physique, and severely weathered face and hands, which accentuated his severely neglected appearance. Armand took a deep breath and sighed. He tried to make eye contact with the bagman, but he appeared to be only semi-lucid, quite possibly drunk, on drugs, or intellectually disabled. After asking him his name and a few basic questions, it was clear: the thirty-eight year old man, named Joey Harrington, was on the autism spectrum. Joey's speech and cognitive abilities were clearly impaired. He was one of the many unfortunate souls abandoned by their families and a system that had little interest in allocating funds into adult programs that cater to the less fortunate and those unable to defend themselves.

Armand was appalled, as he asked once again, "Joey, did *you* steal the jewelry box from that bedroom?"

Joey's eyes barely glanced at Armand, then wandered elsewhere, as he replied, "Jew-lee box. *I* have it."

Portman irritably stepped alongside Joey. "He means he *had* it. *We* have it now. You see, Arnolfini, he admits it."

Armand looked at Portman with disdain. "Joey did *not* admit taking it, Portman. He said he has it, or had it. Perhaps someone gave him the empty jewelry box."

Portman didn't like that Armand dropped the honorific title of 'officer.' Not that he liked Arnolfini to begin with, as a jealous streak ran through his veins, abhorring all the adulation the famous P.I. received in the press. With a grunt, he spat, "Joey walked into the bedroom, we all saw that, and we found him holding the box in his hands, Arnolfini! So, in terms *anyone* can understand, we caught him red-handed! You *do* know what red-handed means, *Detective*?"

While Armand stood calmly—staring at the red-hot-headed officer vent about his red-handed suspect—Portman didn't wait for an answer and rattled on, "Listen, I understand he's a bit slow, but that doesn't exonerate him or free him from prosecution of the law. I'm sure the judge will go easy on him, but guilty he is. And maybe a few days in jail will do him some good. He'll be out of the cold and get some free meals. So, actually, I think I'm being a humanitarian here, Arnolfini."

Armand had to finally respond. "Oh, yes, you're all heart and soul, Portman. And I commend you on your impressive detective work. Very conclusive."

Once again, Portman just huffed and rolled his eyes, as he heatedly grabbed Joey by the arm and escorted him out the door, followed by his fellow policemen.

Armand gazed at the curator. "Mrs. Havenshire, time is of the essence. I implore you to gather all of your employees here immediately?"

Mary squinted. "Mr. Arnolfini, I appreciate your concern for that poor, forgotten young man, as my heart goes out to him, as well. It truly does. But I, too, believe he took the jewelry in that box. He's lucid enough to know that valuable items could get him food and clothing. I have no desire to press charges, yet the missing jewelry is not only quite valuable, Mr. Arnolfini, but also historic artifacts. So, perhaps the food and shelter Joey will receive in jail will be of great benefit to him."

"Mrs. Havenshire, I think a homeless shelter would be more appropriate than a jail cell. Joey was indeed found carrying the box, but where is the jewelry? If it wasn't on his person, where did he stash it? If anything, Joey would have ditched the box and kept the jewelry, if in fact his objective was to acquire something of monetary value. So, there are many unanswered questions here, and he very well might have had an accomplice, or rather a mastermind, who orchestrated this theft. So, if you seriously wish to hire me, it's imperative to assemble your employees here *immediately*, as most museum theft cases are inside jobs. So, *please*, will you humor me?"

Mary glanced at Andrea, who nodded, indicating that she'd be wise to do so. Havenshire conceded.

Minutes later, the employees lined up, and Armand entered a small adjacent office, where he questioned them individually, in private. First up was Sheri Goldman, a stout woman of about forty-five with long brown hair, wearing a stylish pants suit.

"So, Sheri, tell me—do you know anything about this theft?"

Sheri took her seat, looked up at Armand, and shook her head. "No. I'm just the accountant here, Detective." She glanced at the cold, brick office walls around her. "I'm in this main office building all the time, Detective, and never go into the Twain house."

"Never?" Armand asked. "You mean the great Mark Twain never aroused your curiosity enough to venture into his home?"

Sheri shrugged sincerely, unimpressed. "I hate to admit it, but Twain never appealed to me. I'm a Jane Austen fan, myself. Do you realize that Mark Twain married into money, setting himself up for a life in comfort?"

Armand nodded. "Yes, but his talents were far more valuable than whatever money he came into, Mrs. Goldman. And those talents weren't acquired from his in-laws, they were pure, unadulterated Twain—*gold*, in their own way."

Sheri shrugged. "Whatever. I still prefer Jane Austen." Fumbling with her pocketbook, she emphasized, "I'm an accountant, Detective. So this is just a job for me. I don't care whose house is on these grounds."

"I guess that's understandable," Armand said, as he paced before her. "Did you happen to see or hear anything suspicious today?"

"No," she uttered as she pulled out a nail file and seesawed it across her painted nails. "I just crunch numbers here, Detective, all day long. So, I rarely get involved with the historic nuances here or even with most of the staff." Her eyes fixated on an uneven nail and dove into it with her file. "I sit in my little cubicle and do my work. That's it." Finally gazing up at Arnolfini, she added, "I have two children to support and a deadbeat ex, Detective, so I keep focused on my own problems."

Armand nodded. "I see. I'm sorry to hear about your personal difficulties. Thanks for your time, Mrs. Goldman. You may go." He craned his neck toward the door. "Next!"

In walked Benjamin Strathmore, a gray-haired man of about sixty-seven, who sat in Sheri's vacated seat. He announced his name, then said, "I've read about you in the papers, Mr. Arnolfini. You've solved some very interesting art-related crimes. I really loved the case about—"

"Thank you, Mr. Strathmore," Armand cut in, "I appreciate the compliment, but let's not talk about me. Tell me about yourself and what you do here."

"Ah, yes of course," he replied as he fastidiously fixed his uneven collar and fumbled with his necktie. "I'm one of six tour guides here. However, due to the eight inches of snow we had last night and the closed streets, half of our staff didn't come in today."

Armand nodded thoughtfully. "Ah, so there's only a skeleton crew on today. And what about visitors? Did you have many today?"

Benjamin sat upright. "Not at all, sir. Very light. It can get quite boring on days like today." His eyes widened. "Except for when there's been a theft, of course!"

"Yes, Mrs. Havenshire told me the missing jewelry amounts to about eighty-thousand dollars."

Benjamin's head recoiled. "Wow! Eighty Gs! I didn't realize that little box contained such a nice bounty. It only had three pieces in it."

Armand looked deeper into Benjamin's eyes. "So, you knew how many pieces were in the box?"

Benjamin took a defensive posture. "Now wait a minute! Of course I knew. I'm a tour guide, and know every item presented in that house. You don't think *I* took it, do you?"

Armand raised his hand. "Calm down, Benjamin. I'm not accusing you of anything. You must realize that everyone who works here is a possible suspect. But, as the law states, you're all innocent until proven guilty. So, tell me, what were the three pieces of jewelry?"

Benjamin hesitated, then said, "Two rings, both silver, one of which was rather ornate, and a gold pocket watch, engraved with his name." He paused in thought, then added, "Hmm, that watch must be the mother lode, having his name on it. Am I right?"

"I wouldn't know, but I imagine so. It's the piece *I* surely would want most. How about you?"

Benjamin was about to answer, then stopped. "I prefer not to say, Mr. Arnolfini. Are you trying to lure me into admitting something? Because I didn't do it."

"Of course you didn't."

Benjamin smiled. "Do you mean that?"

Armand shook his head. "Of course not. Everyone always says they're innocent, at least at first, Mr. Strathmore."

After several more questions, Armand relieved Benjamin and summoned the next employee. In walked Lucas Raimos, the twenty-four-year old maintenance man, who offered his name and position.

"So, tell me, Lucas, do you know anything about this theft?"

Lucas ran his hand over his prematurely bald head. "Can't say I do, Inspector, other than poor ol' Joey got nabbed."

Armand ignored the incorrect label and said, "So, you know Joey?"

Lucas shrugged. "Not *know* him, like a friend. You know, just from his hanging around the streets and all. I feel sorry for the dude."

Armand nodded. "I hear you. It *is* sad. Unfortunately, a lot of disabled people are abandoned after they age out of their programs at twenty-one, and are left to walk the streets like human refuse."

"Yeah, so I usually try to help him out whenever I can, like this morning."

"What do you mean, this morning? What did you do for him?"

Lucas sat upright in his seat, prideful yet cautious, as his eyes glanced back at the doorway. "Well, especially on cold days like this, I let Joey into the building to thaw out, you know, and even give him some candy or a bag of chips. He loves those hot potato chips. I don't know how the hell he eats them spicy things, but he can down four bags in the blink of an eye."

Armand smiled. "That's awfully nice of you, Lucas."

"Yeah, someone's gotta lend a helping hand, right?"

"For sure," Armand said. "So, do you let him walk through the Twain house by himself?"

Lucas's eyebrows pinched. "Hell, no! I usually hang with him for twenty minutes or so, then have to let him out." Lucas craned his neck to look toward the doorway once again, then back at Armand, as he whispered, "I'm really not supposed to do that, you know. So, you won't tell Mrs. Havenshire, will you?"

Armand shook his head. "I won't say a word, unless it warrants it. Did you accidentally lose sight of Joey, even for a minute or two today? After all, he was caught on video walking into Twain's bedroom, alone."

Lucas sank in his seat, his eyes shifting nervously, then he gazed up at Armand. "Please, don't tell on me. I had to take a leak, but it was only for a minute, I swear. And that's when poor Joey must have gone into the room and stolen the jewelry box."

"How did Joey know jewelry was in there to begin with, or that it was valuable?"

Lucas cracked a smile. "Oh, Joey may be slow, but he knows money. He knows he can eat and feed his belly with moolah, Inspector. I can vouch for that."

Armand corrected him about his proper title, and asked, "So, tell me, when you came out of the bathroom, where was Joey at that time?"

"Don't know for sure, Detective. That's when I lost him. I walked around the entire house, looking for him, but he was gone. It must have been twenty minutes later when the police arrived. They found Joey walking the street with the box in his hand. Poor Joey didn't know any better, and walked right into their trap."

Armand paced the room, then turned back toward Lucas. "So, it's a simple case of an autistic young man swiping a jewelry box, all because you went to the bathroom while trying to be a Good Samaritan. Is that it?"

Lucas nodded. "That's about it, sir. I didn't tell the police I let Joey in the building, or that I foolishly took a leak and lost him. But it was all an innocent mistake. I guess they'll feed and shelter him for several days and release him, right? That's what the officer said."

"There's no telling what they'll do, Lucas. However, you've overlooked one main concern—the jewelry is still missing, eighty-thousand dollars' worth."

Lucas's eyes sprang open. "Eighty grand!?" He squinted, then blurted, "I thought it was worth ten grand, max."

Armand peered deep into his young eyes. "Who told you ten grand?"

Lucas shifted in his seat, his eyes darting left and right. "I-I don't remember."

"Oh, sure you do, Lucas. It evidently annoyed you to hear that it's worth a hell of a lot more than ten thousand dollars. Were you cheated out of your cut?"

Lucas grabbed both sides of the seat, firmly. "I don't know what you mean, or what you're insinuating, but I had nothing to do with this! *Joey* stole the jewelry. The police caught him and the surveillance video verified that! So why all these questions?"

"Here's what *I* think, Lucas. I think someone who knew the true value of jewelry in that box roped you into this scheme. And they cheated *you*, big time! They made you out to be a chump, Lucas. A stupid, little chump. Meanwhile, Joey was just the scapegoat, the poor soul who can't defend himself. So, tell me, what did they do? Split the money with you, giving you a measly five grand, while they made off with seventy-five thousand big ones? Think of that, Lucas, *seventy-five grand!*"

Lucas's face glowed like a red-hot chili pepper as he exploded, "That bitch! That money-hungry bitch! I was going to give her eight grand to help with raising her kids." His eyes rolled in furious circles. "I can't believe her! You try to do something nice, and this is what you get. Pissed on!" He finally looked up at Armand. "You know what I mean? I figured Joey would be set free, or at least get some food and shelter. She would get some dough that her no-good ex never coughs up, and all *I* wanted was two grand for my services."

"Well, perhaps the court will go easy on you, Lucas. But you really got yourself into a jam. So, you instructed Joey to take the jewelry box, and then what, give the rings and watch to you?"

Lucas's lips twisted with frustration. "Yeah, but I immediately ran and gave it to *her*, that calculating bitch! She makes me sick!"

Armand already knew who "she" was, but wanted other answers. "So, I assume the video cutting out really was due to the weather?"

"Yeah, an unlucky break," Lucas moaned as he shook his head. "I wanted it all recorded on video. You know, open and shut case. But, the police didn't seem to care—they caught him with the box. That was good enough for them." He paused; looked down at the floor, then back up at Armand. "Is that why you hung around here, questioning all of us?"

Armand nodded. "It didn't make sense. If the video showed Joey taking it, I *might* have conceded to the idea. But it caused serious doubt, enough to dig deeper."

Lucas glanced out the window at the snowflakes wafting on the cold breeze. "All because of a temporary outage and a nosy detective. What luck."

"Well, to be honest, once I found out it was an autistic person, I had serious reservations. Yes, many understand the value of money, but how would they know how to hock it in order to cash out? Unless they were in cahoots with someone, or were very high-functioning, which Joey wasn't." Armand placed his hand on Lucas's shoulder. "Now, it's time to tell me, where is the jewelry?"

A tear welled in Lucas's eye and his throat constricted, as remorse gripped him. "I gave it to Sheri. It must be in her office somewhere."

Armand turned and called for Mrs. Havenshire, who walked in with Andrea. Armand pointed to Lucas and relayed the whole story.

Mrs. Havenshire looked at Lucas and shook her head. "I never expected such behavior from *you*, Lucas. You're a good-hearted soul. But you were misled and committed a terrible crime, despite your noble intentions." As Lucas's eyes shamefully peered down at the floor, she added, "You cannot do right by doing wrong, Lucas. Now, let's go see Sheri!"

The foursome marched down the hall to Goldman's office and walked in. Sheri looked up from her desk and nearly choked, as the blood in her face fled, leaving her as pale as the statue of Mark Twain in the vestibule. By the looks on all their faces, especially the twisted one of betrayal on Lucas's, Sheri knew darn well what they wanted. Yet, she couldn't bring herself to come clean, as she uttered, "Can I help you?"

"You sure can, Sheri!" Lucas blurted. "You can cough up the *eighty*-grand worth of jewelry I gave you, you greedy snake!"

Sheri just closed her eyes, as her head fell into the palms of her hands, which at least sported nicely filed nails.

Having solved the case, Armand bid Mary and the staff farewell and escorted Andrea out into the cold once again. They hopped into his flashy '37 Cord and plowed through the snow and slush back to her apartment.

As Andrea reheated their dinner, Armand put on the refined, symphonic-rock of Renaissance. As Annie Haslam's velvety voice hovered over the sophisticated rhythms and lush, symphonic swells of the music, Armand and Andrea retook their seats. They gazed deeply into each other's eyes. Clinking their flutes once again, they celebrated their six-month anniversary amid the warm glow of a romantic fire.

THE YOKO, OH NO! MYSTERY

"Painting to Hammer a Nail"
by Yoko Ono

Armand Arnolfini beeped the horn of his '57 Ford Thunderbird coupe for the third time. With a stupefied smile, he even waved at Andrea St. John to get her attention as she stood on the sidewalk in front of Penn Station.

Andrea turned toward the strange, yellow Thunderbird once again, but couldn't detect the annoying, strange man beeping the horn due to the glare on the windshield. Irritably, she twisted her lips and continued to scan the streets for Armand's iconic '37 Cord.

Armand finally rolled down the window and yelled, "Hey, gorgeous! Care for a ride in my classic sports car?"

Tetchily, she turned and retorted, "*No!* My boyfriend is..." she did a double-take as she squinted, then laughed, finally recognizing it was Armand. "I thought you were a nagging flirt, trying to pick me up."

Armand chuckled as he took off his sunglasses. "Well, in that case, I'm glad you refused the offer." He hopped out, ran to the curbside, and opened the passenger door.

"What's this?" she said as she walked toward the car. "A new toy?"

"I guess you can say that. Isn't she a beauty?"

Andrea rolled her eyes and giggled. "You're something else." Her eyes scanned the old sports car's sleek lines and vibrant yellow color, then she slipped into her seat.

As Armand got behind the wheel once again, Andrea surveyed the retro dashboard and added, "Well, at least you're getting closer, Armand. Now you're only twenty-eight years behind the times."

"Ah, come on! You work at a museum, for goodness sake. You should be accustomed to old, *classy* things," he said with a smile as he brushed a piece of lint off his posh Brioni suit.

Andrea's face lit up with a warm smile as she reached over and grasped his hand tenderly. "You're right, I do love *old*, classy things. You *and* this car are quite exquisite."

Armand chuckled. "You're very funny for an old lady *my age*. I guess that's why I'm attracted to you—I love antiques." Before she could respond, he leaned over and kissed her on the lips, while "Head Over Heels" by Tears for Fears played on the radio. He leaned back. "And, by the way, you're a pretty fantastic find, far more precious than all of the priceless artwork I've rescued from oblivion."

As she beamed, Armand shifted the Thunderbird into gear and pulled out. He glanced at her. "Now, for another surprise. Before going to see *Tosca* at the Met, we'll be eating dinner at Barbetta. It's the oldest Italian restaurant in Manhattan. It was founded in 1906 by Sebastiano Maioglio.

And get this—it's still owned by the family, namely his daughter, Laura."

Andrea nodded. "Impressive. But how do you know all of this?"

As Armand swerved and beeped the horn at a taxi driver who cut him off, he replied nonchalantly, "I know Laura. She also was an Art History major."

Andrea gripped the dashboard then quickly buckled her seatbelt. She looked at him with a suspicious eye. "Just how well do you know her?"

Armand glanced at her and chuckled. "Andrea, she's a heck of a lot older than us. I mean, I love antiques, but seriously, are you jealous?"

Andrea held on tight as Armand speedily weaved in and out of traffic like a true New Yorker. As Andrea swayed to and fro, she said, "Well, we've only been dating eight months, and we're not kids ourselves, Armand, even though you drive like one!"

Armand laughed. "What can I say, I have young blood and a need for speed and adventure." His eyes glanced in his rear-view mirror as he quickly shifted lanes. "But as for Laura, sweetheart, she's probably twenty years older than us, in her fifties, I believe."

"Armand, you'll be forty next month."

"Hey! Don't rush my age," he said with a smile. "Okay, so perhaps she's only twelve years older, but still older."

Andrea took a deep breath, relieved to hear of Laura's older age, as she tried to conceal her sigh. "Oh, I wasn't jealous, honey. Besides, I wouldn't want to swell that handsome head of yours, now would I?"

Armand glanced at her. "Yes, why would you, since you already did. And I have strict rules—I only allow *one* head-swelling compliment per evening."

Andrea chuckled her apprehensions away as she said, "Well, you certainly deserve more than one. Anyhow, I look forward to meeting her."

Having parked the car and entered the midtown restaurant, they were cordially greeted by Laura Maioglio, who took the couple on a mini tour. She pointed out how she had redecorated the establishment back in 1962 with imported Italian artifacts, turning it into an elegant, first-class Italian restaurant with the look of an 18th century Piemonte palazzo. During the tour Laura and Armand reminisced about their first meeting and their shared love of art and art history, while Andrea grew more captivated by Laura's knowledge and charm with each new revelation.

As a museum curator, Andrea always loved being in the company of interesting people, especially women *older* than Armand. Deep down, she knew Armand had been a fervently faithful husband to his wife, even six years after her death, and that the problem wasn't with him, but rather with her. Andrea had previously been engaged to Ron Siler, a courtship that had lasted five years. Two days before the wedding, she had returned to their apartment early, having forgotten her purse, and found Ron in bed with her best friend. Having lost both her lover and best friend, Andrea was devastated, wounded too deeply to heal. At least, that is, until she met Armand.

As Andrea looked at him now, it became clear: the more she was getting to know him, the more she realized how foolish she had been in the car and how special he was.

Laura escorted the couple to their table and motioned to her waiter. As she pulled out the chair for Andrea, she looked at Armand. "I have a brand new antipasto I made especially for you both. It's on me."

As Andrea took her seat and Armand thanked her, Laura looked at Andrea. "I'm glad to see Armand has finally started dating again, especially with someone he speaks so highly of. And the fact that you're an attractive young lady doesn't hurt, either."

Andrea blushed. "Thank you, Laura." Her head swung around to scan the elegant 18th century ambiance. "And you've done a magnificent job redecorating. It's quite impressive. I have a special affinity for the past."

Laura nodded graciously. "Thank you. And, yes, Armand has told me that you're the curator of the *Barnum Museum*." She chuckled. "And about his hunt to find your long-lost mermaid. A very *ugly* mermaid, I was told."

Andrea giggled. "Yes, the Feejee mermaid *is* quite hideous, but a great find." She glanced admiringly at her lover, then back at Laura. "Armand saved another fine piece of American history. That single attraction boosted our ticket sales quite significantly. In fact, the Feejee mermaid has already quadrupled Armand's finder's fee."

Armand's eyes widened. "Ah! So now you tell me. I knew I charged you too little." He looked up at Laura. "That's what I get for letting my enamored heart rule my mouth during our negotiations." He looked back at Andrea with loving eyes. "But I couldn't think of a more beautiful woman that I'd sell my soul for."

As Andrea's face glowed with a radiant smile, Laura glanced at Armand's passionate gaze, then back at Andrea's vibrant expression. The electricity between the couple was almost blinding. "You're a very fortunate couple. I haven't seen such magnetism since the days when John and Yoko sat at this very table."

Andrea's face paled at the thought of John's tragic demise, which Laura immediately noticed. "I'm sorry, Andrea," she said as she grasped her hand reassuringly. "I certainly didn't mean to revisit the horror of John's death. It's just that Armand and I had some wonderful moments with the two of them. And if you saw the love they shared for each other, you'd know what I mean. It truly was intense, a harmonious oneness." She looked at Armand. "Right?"

Armand nodded pensively. "Yes, despite their brief breakup, they were destined for each other." He looked at Andrea. "I wish you could have met him, he was a spectacular man. Despite some rough periods in his youth, John was a loving husband and father, a wise and inspirational philosopher, and needless to say, a musical genius."

Andrea managed to smile. "Yes, I truly would have loved to have met him." Her eyes gazed up at Laura, then veered back at Armand. "But what about Yoko? I don't doubt they loved one another, but the rumors have always blamed her for tearing apart the Beatles." Her eyes veered between both of them. "Is there any truth in that?"

Laura shrugged and uttered, "Well, just listen to George Harrison's song 'While My Guitar Gently Weeps.' I think that sums up how the band felt about Yoko's invasion into their world."

"I hate to say it, but I really didn't pay much mind to the lyrics," Andrea confessed.

"Well, the lyrics were aimed at John, as one verse says, 'I don't know how someone controlled you. They bought and sold you,'" Laura suggested. "While another says, 'I don't know how you were diverted. You were perverted, too.' They're really quite powerful words. Sad, actually. It was a tough time for all of them, especially when Yoko sat in on their recording sessions. I heard she even tried to give them advice about songwriting. I would have loved to be a fly on the wall during *those* sessions."

Andrea squinted pensively, as Armand chimed in, "The way I saw it, The Beatles had already been going through a rough patch. There was friction between all of them. Yet, not so much with Ringo, who was often said to be the peacekeeper. But it was simply a natural progression of life. When close buddies reach an age when they start dating, their interests and passions are drawn to their girlfriends and wives, over their friends. Even in a family environment, when one sibling gets married first, the others feel slighted, devalued, hurt. That's when jealousy rears its ugly head. John even addressed the issue in his song 'Jealous Guy.'"

Andrea glanced down at the table, knowing all too well about the dangers of jealousy. As the waiter placed a robust dish of hot and cold antipasto on the table, Laura said, "Well, I'll leave you both to enjoy your dinner." Before she took her leave, she added, "You should tell Andrea about your mysterious Yoko Art Case. I'm sure she'll enjoy that, too."

Andrea drew her attention back to Armand, who nodded slowly, thoughtfully. He jabbed at a piece of mozzarella while she harpooned a roasted pepper. "Well?" she asked. "I'd love to hear it."

As they each took a small bite of their appetizers, Armand chewed mechanically, deep in thought, then swallowed. His eyes drifted up to hers. "Very well. But personally, I call it the *Yoko, Oh No! Mystery*." As Andrea squinted, he continued, "It was several months after—what the papers termed—my *Russian Link Case*. It was about five years ago. I believe it was December 5th of 1980. That's when I had finally accepted Yoko's invitation to attend one of her gallery exhibits in SoHo."

"What do you mean by *finally* accepted?"

Armand shrugged. "Well, as you know, my forte and love for art resides mostly in the genres of realism and surrealism. I'm not one for most branches of modern art. I do like some pieces, but overall, it's not my cup of tea..." he glanced around. "Or espresso."

Andrea chuckled, as he continued, "Anyhow, I had strolled into *New Horizons Gallery* that evening, and thus begins my tale."

†††

As I walked in, John Lennon graciously greeted me. "Armand, my pal, I'm awfully glad you could make it." He craned his neck to see if he could locate his wife. "I know Yoko will be pleased you showed up. To have a noted art connoisseur like *you* present is pretty cool."

"It's my pleasure, John," I said with a genuine yet awkward smile.

Admittedly, I felt a bit guilty, knowing that my tastes differed significantly from his wife's. Yet, as my eyes veered away from John's sharply chiseled features, they inevitably landed on an array of bland displays mixed in with works from two other abstract expressionists, which were incoherent splashes of color on large canvases. The abstractionists always seemed to paint on colossal canvases, as if that would give greater meaning to nothingness. I tried my best to conceal my bewilderment and embarrassment, the latter, not so much for me as for *them*, the so-called *artists*.

While locked in my uncomfortable gaze, I suddenly felt a hand grab mine. I broke my gaping stare and turned to see Yoko, who smiled and led me to one of her exhibits. There before me stood a little white box on a white pedestal.

I looked at her. "What is it supposed to be?"

She looked at me with a peculiar expression, as if I were dense. She pointed to the box's cover. "Well, read it."

I leaned closer. It read: *A BOX OF SMILE Y.O. '71.*

I looked at her and nodded slightly. "Oooh, okay. I guess you made this in 1971."

She shook her head, exasperated, yet chuckled. "Open it, silly!"

Again, my eyes couldn't conceal my bewilderment as I replied, "Oh! You mean *I* can *touch* your artwork?"

"Of course, Armand. The role of the artist must change. It can no longer be all about me, me, me. I wish to include you…" She turned and pointed to a teenaged girl standing nearby. "And *you!*" Then she turned toward three men and pointed at each of them. "And *you*, and *you*, and *you!*" she said, having included everyone presently standing before her work of art.

"Okay, if you say so," I replied as I approached her white box and opened the lid. No big surprise, the empty box had a mirror in its base, thus revealing my own smile. Well, in this case, it wasn't so much a smile as it was a squint and a twisted lip of disappointment. Unfortunately, I had failed to condition myself before arriving that night, as all my cordial pretenses were left at home.

Naturally, Yoko noticed my expression. "You don't like it?"

I tried to muster a smile out of friendship, and perhaps pity, but an awkward contortion swept over my face, which, although looking silly, did not amount to a pleasant smile. "I must be honest, Yoko. I don't understand this whole revolution by the avant garde to make a mockery of tradition, or to spurn the many years of hard work that artists must struggle through in order to acquire the skills necessary to create compelling works of art."

Before she could respond, I added, "But, that's only my personal opinion. I'm sure you have plenty of admirers. So I apolo—"

"She certainly *does* have admirers!" a rotund man irritably interjected.

A teenage girl chimed in, "You're just an old fogey, mister."

The man with round glasses and a crew cut huffed and shook his head. "That's for damn sure! Why do Neanderthals like you even bother to come to enlightening events like this? You're a real downer, mister."

Before I could answer, Yoko politely did so for me. "He's a friend and was invited here. So, please, don't take it out on him."

With that, the hefty man and man with glasses glanced at me and huffed. The young girl shook her head and left the gallery, while the other man—who had remained silent—caught my eye and rolled his eyes in disgust at the avant-garde crowd. Then, he, too, walked away. Meanwhile, the two stone-faced gentlemen stared at me with dagger-eyes, as if I were Adolf Eichmann standing trial. To say I felt uncomfortable would be an understatement. I was clearly out of my element, and I had insulted a dear friend without the chance to apologize and explain my stance further.

As I looked at Yoko, John strolled over. "What seems to be the trouble?" He glanced at the white box. "You're all supposed to be smiling," he said as his trademark grin lit up his precious face.

"I'm afraid I don't understand this type of art, John. And I've insulted Yoko. I apologize. As we all know, art *is* subjective."

John nodded. "Yes. Even my own sis called my song 'Love Me Do' pathetic dribble, or something to that effect." He laughed. "Everything in life is subjective. After all, even Jesus had his doubting Thomas."

I sheepishly looked at Yoko, who, to my surprise, wasn't fazed, and warmly grasped my hand once again. She smiled. "Come, *Thomas*, I'll convert you, sooner or later."

As we both walked toward another exhibit, I had to respond truthfully, as is my disposition. "Well, *this* Thomas doubts it. But I'm always open to see and assess new things, Yoko."

✝✝✝

Andrea shook her head as she put a melon wrapped with prosciutto on her plate. "That was a bit rude, Armand. I can't believe you spoke to Yoko like that."

Armand chewed and swallowed a Sicilian olive and wiped his mouth. "Andrea, I learned to be discerning from my father. As a curator, he had to make judgment calls all the time at the *Uffizi Gallery* in Florence. Works by lesser-known artists had to be truthfully evaluated using the guidelines of the trade. Just as an athlete gets evaluated and judged, so, too, must an artist. And not everyone makes the grade. Everyone can't be a professional athlete, musician, artist, or even a winner. I see the world becoming far too lenient with such matters, and soon everyone will be given a trophy just for being alive and breathing. I hope that day never comes, Andrea, but hard decisions must be made if we ever intend to maintain and improve our high standards, laudable values that brought Western civilization to this glorious summit on which we're all fortunate enough to stand on."

Just then, the waiter cleared the plates and took their orders for the main course. Armand took a deep breath and continued with his story…

✝✝✝

Yoko then led me to her *Painting to Hammer a Nail* display. It consisted of a blank white canvas hanging on a wall with a real hammer tied to it. Off to the side was a tin bucket mounted to the wall.

Once again, I stopped and stared at the display, not getting the gist of its purpose. I looked at Yoko with a sheepish smile. "I'm sorry—what are you trying to say here?" I raised my hand. "Wait! Allow me to guess. I'm supposed to use your blank canvas, aka the painting, to hammer in a nail, as if it's a real hammer. Right?"

"You're taking the title too literally, Armand," Yoko said. "Or rather, just not reading it properly."

Before she could explain, the two men from the previous display had followed us to this exhibit, whom I silently labeled Himmler and Goering, not only due to their earlier Gestapo-like scolding, but they actually exhibited similar physical traits. One was weaselly with a crew cut, round spectacles, and was very well dressed; the other was very plump and squeezed into a white suit, looking like a stuffed weisswurst.

Himmler peered into the tin bucket, which was full of nails. He grabbed a nail and looked at Yoko. "May I?"

Yoko grinned, happy that someone truly understood her artwork, as the man—now elated to join in Yoko's creation—grasped the hammer hanging by the blank painting and drove a nail into the white canvas.

"Excellent!" Yoko said as she then turned toward me. "Now do you see? It's a 'Painting to Hammer a Nail!'"

This time I laughed as I shook my head. It *was* kind of cute. But as is my nature, I had to be honest. "Well, Yoko, technically speaking, it's not even a painting—it's a blank, white canvas. So the title is a bit misleading." I glanced back at the canvas, now with a nail driven into it, then back at her. "But I'm getting the gist of your participatory type of artwork, which I would categorize as Arts and Crafts, not Fine Art. But that's just me. I'm sorry."

Yoko didn't take offense and playfully shoved me, as John caught me from behind and warmly wrapped his arm around my shoulders. "Making a bit of sport with me wife,

Sport, ay?" he said wittily. As I chuckled, John walked me to the small bar near the front entrance and ordered us drinks. The three of us spoke for hours about art, music, and life.

John was elated that after five years of hibernation, he finally released the album, *Double Fantasy,* which was already garnering praise and hitting the top of the charts. He was amused at how the hit song, "(Just Like) Starting Over" nicely summed up the resurrection of his musical career—a new chapter had begun.

Our conversion then veered back to art, and Yoko mentioned how one of her mentors, John Cage, had influenced her. Cage was a radical composer/artist who penned the musical piece entitled 4′33″—to be performed in three movements. However, the musicians were instructed not to play their instruments at all. Hence, the effect was silence, or rather, the sounds listeners might hear during that silence.

I was beginning to understand where these "artists" were all heading; namely, not in the direction of building upon solid artistic foundations of aesthetics, technique, and subject matter, but rather in the visionary direction of veering off that path, to abandon all known foundations, and to think of ideas that were different from the norm.

Although I still couldn't bring myself to term such endeavors as High Art or even Fine Art—believing theses musical and paint-less gimmicks to be thought experiments, while others were cheap publicity stunts, such as Marcel Duchamp's print of Mona Lisa with a mustache—I did see a need for venturing into uncharted territories of the mind. I believe the term *Conceptual Works* would be more apropos than Abstract Art or any other term that included the word 'art' itself.

After all, Duchamp was a pioneer in the early twentieth century, and was credited for establishing the *Anti-Art* movement, where he utilized ready-made objects, such as the porcelain urinal he entered into the Society of Independent Artists Exhibition in 1917, which created a stir in the art world.

As I told John and Yoko, if the roots of most forms of modern art emanated from a philosophy of *Anti-Art*, I believed I was justified in not appending the word *art* to these movements. They smiled and offered no answer, but the wheels were certainly turning in their heads. However, in all honesty, I found our discussions enlightening, and could appreciate the avenues innovators were taking in various forms of expression. It was a splendid evening.

†††

As the waiter delivered both entrées, Andrea looked at Armand. "I see the doubting Thomas was starting to come around, but still held on to his convictions."

Armand picked up his fork and spoon and twirled a spindle-full of linguini on his fork, then dipped it into the *Fra Diavolo* fish sauce. He looked up. "As I told you, honey, people should be honest with one another. It doesn't have to get ugly and confrontational. They could either accept it or reject it. Personally, I think it's better than lying." With that, he inserted the ball of tasty linguini into his mouth.

"I suppose so," Andrea conceded. "But when dealing with eminent figures such as John and Yoko, I guess, well… I guess *I* wouldn't have the nerve to be so candid. I'd try to couch my opinions a bit." She cut into her chicken Marsala, took a quick taste, and prodded, "So, where is this mysterious art case that Laura spoke of? Swallow that pasta, *Sport*, and let's go!"

"Okay, okay," he said, smiling at her imitation of Lennon's expression. "Just as we should *Give Peace a Chance*, please give *me* a chance to eat some of this great food." He took several more mouthfuls—making sure they all contained an assortment of shrimp, mussels, and clams with the pasta—then leaned back, rubbed his stomach, and continued his tale.

†††

John, Yoko, and I hadn't kept track of the time—being so engrossed in our conversations—that we each flinched and turned when the curator started to shut off the lights.

As the rear galleries went dark, Yoko looked at us. "Excuse me, I want to see my works once more before we leave. They're like my other babies." With that, she ran back, while John and I continued to talk as we walked toward the front door.

As I reached for the doorknob, we heard a scream! John and I spun around to see Yoko run toward us, wide-eyed and frantic. "Someone stole my *Painting to Hammer a Nail*!"

Flabbergasted, we all rushed to the rear gallery in question, and—as sure as my earlier blank stare—there before us was a blank wall. Even the tin bucket of nails was gone. As John embraced Yoko to console her, I looked at the curator. "Who was the last person in this gallery?"

Ruefully, he shook his shoulders. "I'm so sorry. I don't know. I was busy speaking with two major clients in the adjacent gallery."

"Does this place have a rear exit?" I asked.

"Yes," he said, in a nervous higher octave. "But it's blocked with crates. Several exhibition pieces arrived late this morning, so we didn't have a chance to clear a path."

I turned toward John and Yoko, who approached us; the four of us now being the only ones left in the building. "Did any of you notice who the last people to leave the gallery were?"

The curator bit his lips. "Again, I'm sorry. I was tied up in conversation. Once everyone left, that's when I started turning off the lights."

Meanwhile, John and Yoko wracked their brains, trying to remember, when John said, "Actually, one bloke was that odd-looking chap. You know, the one who drove the nail into Yoko's painting."

Yoko's eyes lit up. "Yes! He loved my work." She looked at me. "Do you think he stole it?"

"It's far too early to say, Yoko. We need to know who was here tonight." I looked at the curator. "I saw a guest book on the front table, where even I signed in. Let's cross-check that with Yoko's invitation list."

"Right!" he said, while Yoko ran and retrieved her guest list out of her handbag.

We placed them side-by-side and went down the list. As we did, I said, "Bear in mind, the thief most likely didn't sign in, or possibly entered a false name. But this is a starting point. Perhaps one of these attendees saw who walked out of that gallery last." I looked at Yoko. "How did you gather this list?"

"Actually, it was given to me by Mark Rothko, before he died."

"So I take it they were all his fans?"

"Well, most of them were. Others were harvested from his artist friends and gallery owners to build his base. Naturally, I added my followers to the list, as well."

I squinted. "I'm not too familiar with modern art, but I assume Rothko's collectors generally purchased abstract expressionist works, right?"

"Not necessarily," Yoko said. "Mark never wanted to be classified, or pigeon-holed. Others labeled Rothko as an abstract expressionist."

"Okay, but generally speaking, his and your list is comprised of collectors of modernist works, which narrows down our demographic. If the culprit is not on your list, he or she may be on a similar modern artist's list."

The curator's head popped up. "I remember!" he exclaimed. "Mr. Kraus. He's the man who drove the nail in the canvas."

I looked at him. "His name is on both—Yoko's list and your guest book?"

"No," he said. "Neither. But you said our demographic is collectors of modernist artworks, and I recall him being at my abstract exhibitions in the past."

I rubbed my chin. "So how is it you remembered his name?"

The curator laughed. "Because Kraus in German means 'curly-haired,' and Mr. Kraus has a crew cut—very short, straight hair. The disparity stuck in my head, not to mention that he's an avid admirer and collector of modern art, with strong views on the subject."

"Yes," I said. "I definitely noticed *that*!" Himmler certainly had something to say, all right. "Do you have his contact information?"

"I'm sure it's in one of my old guest books. Give me a minute," he said, as he spun around and darted to his desk.

Meanwhile, Yoko had been scanning the guest book and her list with her finger, when suddenly her hand stopped. She looked up at me. "There are twenty-three names that aren't on my invitation list but *are* in the guest book. All of the guests included their phone numbers and addresses, except for one. It's a Mr. Joseph Brodowski."

I thought to myself, *I wonder if that's fat man Goering?* Then said, "Let's get a telephone book and see if we can find Mr. Brodowski."

Ten minutes later, Yoko located his name and number while the curator excitedly furnished me with Mr. Kraus's phone number. I duly made the calls and asked each to meet me the next day at the gallery, at different times, which they did.

To my surprise, Mr. Brodowski wasn't Weisswurst Goering, but rather the slim man who had silently sided with me during Himmler and Goering's severe tongue-lashings, then slipped away.

"So, Mr. Brodowski, I noticed you appeared to agree with me last night when I voiced my opinion about Yoko's Smile Box. Why was that?"

"It's pretty plain to see why, Mr. Arnolfini. You saw the trash in that gallery. It's an outrage. Just because she's married to a famous Beatle, talentless gallery leeches cater to the artless celebrity and give her exhibit space. It's sickening. How is true talent, like *me*, supposed to get a show?"

"So, you're an artist. What genre?"

"A realist, Mr. Arnolfini. Just like my realist view of life. The rich and their cronies get the limelight, while true talent struggles in the shadows, hoping for a break. I attend many galleries, just to see what these propagandists are peddling, and it's primarily manure. I created better works of art when I was eighteen months old, using my diaper as a palette to smear my feces on the walls."

I had all to do to stifle a chuckle as I said, "Even your sarcasm is artful, Mr. Brodowski. But I can see you harbor a lot of hatred for artists such as Ms. Ono. Did you, by chance, steal Yoko's nail painting out of frustration, or perhaps in retaliation against the art world?"

Joe twisted his lips and shook his head. "Why the hell would I want her trash, Mr. Arnolfini? If I did take it, I'd throw it out. And let's face it, if I threw it on the street, who would even know that it was a valuable work of art by the famous Yoko Ono? It's a blank white canvas with nails in it. There's nothing original or even indicative of Yoko about it. So how can something so common and pathetically ordinary be of great value?"

I shrugged. "I'm not here to evaluate her artwork. As you gathered, I don't fully understand the attraction myself, although I am starting to at least comprehend these artists' motives. But there's been a crime committed, and I've been hired to solve it. So, you deny stealing the painting, even if only to destroy it?"

"Most assuredly! You've got the wrong guy, Mr. Arnolfini."

†††

As Andrea finished her chicken Marsala, she looked up. "I don't know, Armand, this guy has a lot of pent-up anger. And usually, resentment that toxic needs an outlet, like destroying things." She wiped the Marsala sauce off her mouth as the waiter removed her plate and handed her a dessert menu. She looked back at Armand. "Before we get to dessert, you must to continue. I can't be left hanging, I need to know who did it."

Armand glanced at the dessert menu. "Are you sure? They have tiramisu!"

Andrea shook her head. "No, sweetie. Tiramisu is *your* favorite dessert, not mine. Let's get on with the story, shall we?"

Armand reluctantly placed the dessert menu down. "Very well," he said, as he continued...

†††

I then met with Rudolph Kraus an hour later at the gallery. As the Himmler double walked in the door, his beady eyes behind his round glasses widened. "Oh! It's *you*, the artless antagonist."

"If that's what you wish to call someone with a different perspective, fine, Mr. Kraus. Please have a seat."

As he did, his eyes scanned the gallery. "So, why did *you* ask me down here? I thought it was the curator who called, and assumed I would be viewing additional works of art or something otherwise enlightening."

"No. No additional works of art, Mr. Kraus. Yet, I do hope this meeting will be enlightening. I'd like to ask you, which work of art by Yoko did you like the best yesterday?"

Kraus rolled his eyes, not seeing the meaning of this meeting or the question, yet he complied in his stoic, monotone voice, "I liked them all, actually. She has a unique outlook on life. And let's face it; being married to John Lennon certainly boosts the value of her work. A sound investment, wouldn't you say?"

"Perhaps. Would *you* be interested in buying one?"

"Not presently, but perhaps someday. Why? Are you offering a discount or something?"

I laughed. "No. I'm not an art dealer."

Kraus looked at me with a new set of eyes. "Of course you're not. You didn't even like her work. So who are you, and what's this all about?"

"Okay, it's come clean time. I've been hired by Yoko and John to find out who stole her *Painting to Hammer a Nail* last night."

His head recoiled as if electrocuted. "Are you serious? You're questioning *me*? I'm a respected collector! I have three Rothkos, four Hoffmanns, and two de Koonings. Why on Earth would I steal Yoko's work? Your insinuation alone is insulting!" He stood up forcefully. "Where's the curator, or Yoko? I'd like to lodge a formal complaint."

"Mr. Kraus, I didn't accuse you of anything. I've merely asked you some questions."

"You did *not* merely ask me questions. You withheld your identity. That's entrapment! Are you just her friend, or a professional detective?"

"I'm a private investigator. But you're getting quite bent out of shape over this. Are you afraid of being trapped into saying something incriminating?"

"How dare you! You're digging your hole deeper, mister...whatever your name is!"

"You never asked for my name, nor did I falsely state that I was anything other than what I am. You could have asked at any time, but you didn't. So, I didn't mislead you, Mr. Kraus, you simply chose never to ask."

"Fine!" he huffed. "What's your name, Mr. P.I.?"

"My name is Armand Arnolfini. We just wish to solve this case. Did you see anyone suspicious near that painting last night? Or witness someone take it?"

Kraus rolled his eyes. "Of course I didn't see anyone steal it! I would have reported the ratfink immediately. I have a high regard for artwork, as I've told you. I'm an ardent collector. And the only one suspicious last night was *you*—the Neanderthal, out of his time period." His eyes oscillated in thought. "Wait! There was another guy, too— quiet, but certainly vexed. He stood near us. He also seemed out of place."

"Yes, I already spoke with him. He's an artist, but a realist."

"Naturally," Kraus huffed. "It's time for you to be real, Mr. Arnolfini, and end this bogus interrogation. I'm innocent and insulted, as I've stated. So, I'm going to take my leave." With that, he turned and marched out the door.

Yoko walked in from the other room, having listened to both conversations.

I looked at her. "So, do either of them seem suspicious?"

Yoko frowned. "Yes, they both do. One hates me and my work, and the other, although a fan of my work, is quite testy."

"But does one of them give you a nasty, gut-feeling?"

She thought for only a second and said, "Brodowski."

"So, you think he stole your work, for what reason, to destroy it?"

Yoko took a seat next to me, then gazed at me with thoughtful eyes. "No, Armand. Not to destroy my work. Sell it. If he's a starving artist, I'm sure he could use the money." She paused, then muttered. "Actually, I feel sorry for him."

I rested my elbow on the table and plopped my chin into the palm of my hand. I stared out the gallery window at the tall, antiquated buildings in SoHo, with their unique cast-iron façades, then back inside the gallery at all the modern works of art. The juxtaposition of disparate styles was jarring, yet oddly refreshing. The diversity of the human mind *was* something spectacular, something worth celebrating.

I gazed into Yoko's alluring eyes. "Well, you're a goodhearted soul, Yoko, to feel sorry for Brodowski—being that he's a disgruntled, starving artist. But I disagree. Personally, I'd like to see Kraus's art collection, to see if he's lying, or if there's something he's hiding. I'd like you to call him. Tell him you heard he has an impressive collection of abstract pieces, and that you'd love to see them."

Yoko looked at me, not sure if I was heading in the wrong direction, as I added, "And tell him that you'd love to have one of your works in his collection. Furthermore, you'd be open to offering him a special discount, reserved only for avid collectors, like himself. That should nab his curiosity."

†††

Armand couldn't restrain himself from ordering a piece of tiramisu and a cup of cappuccino. As such, Andrea was forced to order her own dessert, opting for an almond tortoni. Moments later, after the waiter delivered their requests, Armand toasted to their special relationship and clinked his cup of cappuccino against her mug of decaf coffee.

Andrea relished the dessert, despite eating it rather quickly, then said, "Okay, you nabbed my curiosity, too, Armand. How about getting back to the case?"

Armand sipped and savored the cappuccino, then took another bite of his tiramisu. He then smiled. "I've made a blunder. I truly didn't realize how this tale would rush my meal." He placed his fork down. "Okay, you win again." And onward Armand went...

†††

Next, Yoko and I took a ride out to Rudolf Kraus' grand estate in Southampton, on Long Island. Naturally, I decided to drive my flashy '37 Cord. Mr. Kraus was instantly enamored with it, being a collector of fine cars himself. However, he had recently sold all of them, including a 1942 Rolls Royce phantom, a 308 GTS Ferrari, and a 1936 Mercedes-Benz 500-K—the latter, I instantly recalled, was the car used by Hermann Goering and Adolf Hitler. Once again, my mind wandered—I still believed Rudy had some sort of bloodline to Heinrich Himmler. *Okay, I jest.* But his physical appearance *was* unnervingly like the *Reichsführer*.

Anyhow, Kraus may have loved my classy old car, but he was not thrilled to see *me*. He had expected only Yoko. I defused that dilemma by explaining we were friends and that I was asked to drive her. With that settled, Yoko, Rudy, and I walked up toward his ultra-modern estate. As we did, I was surprised to see how the lawn and topiary were overgrown and unkempt.

As we entered, however, Yoko and I were deeply impressed. The architecture had a minimalist flair, yet its twenty-foot tall wall of glass overlooking the Atlantic Ocean was breathtaking. Adorning the interior's immense white walls were an array of Rothkos, Hoffmanns, and de Koonings, just as Kraus had stated. Evidently, he hadn't lied, at least not about his art collection, which also included three Calder mobiles hanging from the high ceilings. As we walked into the huge living room, I furtively peeked down the hallways, which appeared to have smaller works of art on those walls, as well.

Meanwhile, Yoko likewise scanned the enormous space, which was as large as the galleries she exhibited in. With modernist works being her cup of tea—or perhaps cup of Gyokuro—Yoko was clearly captivated.

Kraus's disposition, however, was unexpected. He was courteous and hospitable, no doubt due to Yoko's presence, but perhaps because of the ploy I had instructed her to offer. As expected, Kraus took the bait, as he asked, "I'm pleased that you like my collection, Yoko. And yes, I would love to add an Ono to my wall, *if* the price is right."

"Well, Mr. Kraus, few of my works hang on walls," she replied. "I'm an innovator. I shun most existing forms of expression."

Yoko informed Rudy about her noted 1964 performance, called *Cut Piece*—where she had knelt on stage while people from the audience came up and cut pieces of her clothes off.

Just then, I heard a commotion brewing in the kitchen. I looked at Kraus. "Excuse me, but it sounds like you have a problem."

Kraus rolled his eyes and huffed as he made a beeline to the kitchen. Yoko and I followed. As we entered the large—commercial-sized—kitchen, my eyes bulged. There before me was fat-man Goering arguing with a servant. I looked at Himmler. "Of course, you two were at the gallery the other night."

Kraus smirked at me. "Yeah, so what?" His testy attitude had returned. He immediately turned toward Goering. "Wally! Stop this bickering, we have guests."

Wally looked at Rudolph. "I'm sorry, honey, but Jose can be quite trying at times." He looked back at the servant, and commanded, "We'll discuss this *later*!"

Jose looked at Wally with heated eyes and snapped, "I sick 'o dis boolshit! I no get pay in *tres* munths!"

Goering retorted, "I said *shush*! I'll take care of this later."

With that, Jose slammed the crystal decanter down on the marble counter, which shattered. As we all recoiled, Jose cussed under his breath in Spanish and stormed out of the kitchen, leaving behind a mess of dirty plates, half-eaten food, empty wine glasses, and an impressive array of empty or half-finished bottles of top-shelf liquor.

I looked at Hermann Goering, then at Himmler. "I gather you're partners."

Kraus rolled his eyes. "*Lovers*, Mr. Arnolfini. I make no excuses. And I'm sick and tired of being badgered with questions about it!" he barked.

Wally immediately wrapped his arm around him. "Don't let this fool upset you, Rudy." He looked at me with disgust. "I remember *you*. Who the hell are you, and why are you here?"

"My name is Armand Arnolfini. I chauffeured Yoko here to see Kraus's collection, and perhaps to sell him a work of hers, if he's interested."

"*I* handle all acquisitions here, Mr. Chauffeur!" Wally snapped.

Wally pushed himself away from his lover and chided him. "I told you, Rudy, *I'll* handle all of our business affairs." As he continued his scolding, he glanced at Yoko with an agitated glint in his eye. "And you never should have invited Yoko here, not without asking *me* first."

Yoko uncomfortably looked at me. "Perhaps we should go?"

I looked at her. "No, I prefer to stay." I then looked at Wally and Rudolph. "I can see you like throwing lavish parties. You wouldn't be rude enough to kick *Yoko Ono* and her friend out of your house, would you? You know how fast gossip flies."

They glanced at each other apprehensively, then back at me, as Wally said, "You have a sly way of conducting yourself, Mr. Arnolfini, but very well." He turned and irritably walked over to the bar counter. "Can I get either of you a drink?" he asked, without the least bit of hospitality in his voice.

"I'll have a Schnapps, Hermann... I mean Wally."

Wally pivoted around and looked at me strangely. "*Herman*? Where on Earth did you get that name from?"

"No offense," I said. "It surely wasn't Herman Munster, if that's a consolation."

I'm generally not so sarcastic, but there was something off about this Goering look-a-like, and perhaps a little antagonism would elicit more information in the heat of his anger.

"I'll be blunt, Armand," he retorted. "I don't like you!"

"Why should bad blood get between us?" I said. "And never mind the Schnapps. You said you handle all of the business affairs here." I glanced around at their posh mansion. "So, what line of work are you in, Wald-o?"

He looked at me like a raging bull about to charge, then glanced at Kraus, who finally spoke up. "He prefers the name *Wally*, Mr. Arnolfini. And for your information, Wally and I don't work, per se. You see, I inherited all of this. My wife passed away several months ago, and… Well, the police know the whole story, and quite frankly, Wally and I are sick of all the questions. I did *not* kill my wife!"

I flinched at the revelation. "Uh, I never said you did, Rudy. I wasn't aware that your wife died or that there was an on-going investigation."

Kraus sighed, calmly. "Well, I expected you might have known, being that you're a nosy PI, Mr. Arnolfini. But I've always been honest with you and the police. I have nothing to hide. And the same goes for the stolen painting." He looked at Yoko genuinely. "I'd never steal a work of art. I cherish art, Ms. Ono, as I do the artist. I adore talent and beautiful things, and love to be surrounded by them." He looked at Wally lovingly. "And Wally has done an outstanding job of doing that."

I now viewed this Himmler clone with a new set of eyes. I no longer believed him to be the evil chicken farmer who murdered millions, or even Mrs. Kraus, as I turned my gaze toward *Goering*, imagining the man who stole famous works of art during the war to feed his insatiable appetite for beautiful things. However, in this case, Wally was doing it to please his lover. It was time to stick a bigger flame under Goering's fat ass, as I said, "So, Wally, were you upset that Rudy invited Yoko here because *you* stole her artwork?"

That accusation struck Goering's flabby face out of left field, as he twitched with a guilty look that was as clear as glass. He tried to conceal it, as his eyes nervously veered at Kraus, then anywhere but my face. "That's preposterous! You have some hell of a nerve to walk into our house and accuse *me* of stealing her painting." He stepped into the living room and pointed at all the works of art. "I bought all of these masterworks for Rudy. So, tell me, why would I steal a little canvas by Yoko?"

As we all shifted into the living room, I said calmly, "Because you're clearly facing financial difficulties. You might even be broke, and can't afford to buy any more extravagant works."

His face blanched like a white onion, as I slowly peeled away layer after layer of this case.

Wally retorted, "That's absurd!"

Rudy squinted, then looked at his lover. "Wally? *Are* we in financial trouble?"

Anger spread all over Goering's face like the measles as he looked at me with SS-dagger eyes. "You're a damn troublemaker, Arnolfini! Leave! Now!"

Rudy stepped toward Wally. "Answer me!? Are we in financial trouble?"

Wally stood smoldering as he peered right through my eyes into the back of my skull, while Rudy turned toward me, baffled and curious. "And how would *you* know about my financials?"

I looked at Rudy. "Through keen observation—it's what I do." I sat on the arm of a huge leather couch and crossed my arms. "When we pulled up, I noticed the property was badly neglected, evidently for quite some time. And this *is* Southampton—everyone around here gets their lawn and gardens manicured. Then you told me how you, or rather Wally, sold all of your expensive cars. And of course, we all saw how Wally wasn't paying Jose, either." I glanced at Wally, then looked deeply into Rudy's eyes. "I think you need to have a chat with Wald-o about your inheritance, Rudy, if there's even any left."

With that, Wally charged toward me in a fit of rage. "You dirty bastard! You're ruining everything!"

Instinctively, I stood up and grabbed Wally's wrists and twisted them behind his back, holding him tightly. "I knew that would get a rise out of you, Wally, but you've exceeded my expectations."

As Yoko looked on, dazed by the chain of unfolding events, Rudy was utterly taken aback by his lover's gross mismanagement of his finances, as he commanded, "Wally! I entrusted you to handle my estate, eight million dollars' worth. I *demand* to know what's left?"

Meanwhile, Wally continued to struggle in my grip, as he whimpered, "I only tried to please you, Rudy. Look around you. Do you think all those pieces of art are cheap? And what about all the parties you've enjoyed? Entertaining a hundred guests every weekend doesn't come cheap."

Rudy was turning white and started to wobble, as a look of nausea overcame him. Once again, he asked, "How much, Wally? How m-much is left?" he stuttered.

Wally stopped squirming in my arms as his shoulders wilted. His head lowered. A grave look of remorse and shame washed over him, as he mumbled, "I did it all for you, Rudy. I just wanted to make you happy." A slight sniffle could be heard, as he uttered, "We're... broke."

Rudy exploded. "*Broke*! Dear God, Wally! What the hell..." He staggered to the couch and plopped down, rubbing his head as sweat began to bead on his crew-cut scalp. He looked back up at his infuriating and incompetent lover. He was about to scream and chew him out further, but upon seeing Wally's dejected and pathetic face, Rudy's rage turned to resignation. He took a deep breath and sighed.

Rudy now realized he was partially responsible for the fate that had befallen his lover, having overwhelmed him with too many tasks and trusting his poor judgment. He looked at Wally with deep, pensive eyes. "You know I never lie, Wally. So don't lie to Yoko. Did you take her painting?"

Wally ashamedly glanced at Yoko, then at me, then back to Rudy. Again, his head lowered like that of a scolded child. "Last night I noticed how much you loved it, and, well..." He turned and looked at Yoko. "I'm sorry, I'll give it back."

Yoko sighed with relief. "That's okay, Wally. In light of your circumstances," she glanced at Rudy. "I'd like you both to have it."

A painful smile came over Rudy's torn face, mirroring the smile of gratitude on Wally's.

I looked at all of the expensive paintings hanging on the walls, then up at the Calder mobiles, and said, "Perhaps you might want to think about selling some of these to get back on your feet."

Rudy looked up at his prized possessions. "I think you're right, Mr. Arnolfini. I've enjoyed them long enough, and desperate times call for desperate measures." He turned and looked at me. "And I apologize for the way I spoke to you. You sensed, and eventually saw, what I didn't. You're a fine detective." He looked over at Yoko. "And thank you for your generosity and understanding. My partner was very foolish, and this could have gone down a lot differently."

Yoko nodded solemnly. "We all make mistakes, Mr. Kraus. People deserve a second chance. John and I had been separated for well over a year, yet we managed to give it another go. And it's paid off, we're happier than ever. Even his new album is a success. It indeed is just like starting over."

†††

Andrea's face lit up with a warm smile. "Laura was right. That case ended up being an endearing story."

Armand took a final sip of his cappuccino, swallowed it, then sighed, as his brief smile withered into a solemn stare.

Andrea squinted with concern. "What's the matter? Did something else happen?"

A tear welled in Armand's eye. "Well, yes. Two days later was December 8, 1980, the infamous day when Mark Chapman murdered John Lennon."

"Oh, no!" Andrea cried with a heartrending whimper.

"Indeed," Armand replied solemnly. "Now you know why I call it *The Yoko, Oh No! Mystery*."

The Ghent Mystery

Strolling through *The Museum of Fine Arts* in Ghent, Belgium, Armand Arnolfini eagerly took on the role of guide for Andrea St. John, who listened to each of his mini lectures with rapt attention. Andrea's forte centered on artifacts of Americana, being the curator of the *Barnum Museum* in Connecticut, as such, learning about the works of great Flemish masters of the past opened her mind to a whole new world.

As she walked along, she suddenly stopped. She gazed up at *Jupiter and Antiope*. While her eyes scrutinized the two figures in the painting she now felt confident enough to guess whom the artist was, as she turned toward Armand and said, "This one's by Rubens."

Armand gazed at the painting, then back at her. "What makes you say that?"

"Because he loved painting hefty, nude women."

As they both chuckled, Armand shook his head. "Well, that was an astute deduction about Rubens, but this painting happens to be by Anthony van Dyck."

Andrea frowned. "Aw, shucks! I thought I was getting the gist of this."

"Actually, you are, sweetie. Van Dyck was a pupil of Rubens and was deeply influenced by him." Armand glanced back up at the painting. "I'd imagine many people would be fooled into thinking this was a Rubens."

He then escorted her to the painting of *Saint Jerome* by Hieronymus Bosch. "And can you guess who painted this one?" he asked.

Andrea first looked at the pastoral setting, then at Saint Jerome, lying down clutching a crucifix, deep in prayer. She rubbed her chin, then said, "I believe this might be by Hieronymus Bosch."

Armand grinned. "You're a quick learner. To be honest, this isn't in a style that Bosch is most noted for, so how did you deduce that?"

She pointed not at Saint Jerome but at the scenery. "The exotic plants and trees just have his unique signature on them." She leaned in closer. "There's a fantasy-like quality to his works, and this looks similar to the ones you showed me back home in your book."

Armand was truly impressed. "I believe you just might be able to assist me in my art-crime cases one day. You're an excellent student."

"I guess that makes *you* an excellent teacher."

He chuckled and grasped her hand. "But one of the main reasons I picked Belgium for our vacation is the *Ghent Altarpiece* inside the Saint Bavo Cathedral."

With that, he led Andrea outside, then strolled through the crowded cobblestoned streets toward the cathedral. Weaving their way through the throng of people who gathered annually for the famous Ghent Festival, the couple managed to move past mimes, doing their silent acts, various vendors, and even puppeteers, putting on miniature theater for the mass of visitors from all over the world. Attracting, on average, two million people each year, the Ghent Festival was Belgium's equivalent to Germany's Oktoberfest.

Squeezing their way past people eating pretzels, funnel cakes, and drinking beer or wine, the couple managed to enter the large cathedral.

As Andrea instinctively headed for the altar, Armand grasped her hand and drew her back. "It's this way, in the Joos Vijd Chapel."

Andrea squinted. "But you said it's an altarpiece?"

Armand smiled. "Yes, but it's an epic masterpiece and a national treasure, honey. And due to the high volume of spectators, installing it in the chapel was more practical."

As their footsteps echoed off the vacant cathedral's cavernous walls, Andrea glanced around and said, "If it's so monumental, where are all the spectators you've mentioned?"

Armand's shoulders slouched as they approached the chapel. "I guess the frivolities of the festival attract people more than the sublime qualities of fine art. What can I say?"

As they entered the chapel, Andrea's eyes nearly popped out of her head. "You can say...they don't know what they're missing!" she exclaimed as she gasped and stopped in her tracks.

Standing before her was the eleven-feet tall by fifteen-feet wide masterpiece, encased in a modern steel frame and protected behind glass. Created in twelve oak panels, when fully opened, the *Ghent Altarpiece* featured Biblical paintings inside each of its framed sections. The meticulous work by Hubert and Jan van Eyck was a miraculous achievement in Western art, one that stunned the adoring crowd when it premiered in 1432, as well as millions of others throughout the centuries, right up to Andrea now, who stood in awe with an astonished look on her face.

Her eyes scanned the perplexingly realistic scenes and numerous figures, from Jesus seated in a central panel, looking like an imperial pope with His bejeweled vestments, over to Mary and Saint John the Baptist, then to the panels of angels, singing and playing instruments, and finally over to Adam and Eve, each on opposite sides of the huge polyptych.

Andrea was stunned by the realism as she walked closer. "I didn't think artists at this time painted with such precision."

Armand walked beside her. "It truly *is* miraculous, isn't it?"

Andrea couldn't break her eyes away as she stood before the central panel and leaned closer. "Good Lord, the detail in Jesus's face and hands, His vestments and jewels, even the tapestry behind Him, is amazing."

She finally broke her gaze to glance at Armand. "I feel as though I could touch his velvety robe and jewelry, they look so real."

Armand smiled. "I told you you'd be amazed." Yet his plump cheeks soon withered as he looked back at the grand painting. His discerning eyes zeroed in on its defects, the ravages of time and numerous attempts to conserve the masterpiece.

Andrea noticed his expression. "What? What is it?"

Armand's eyes scanned broadly over the entire piece then back to the panel before them. "Unfortunately, this entire work is in desperate need of serious conservation. Do you see all those areas where the paint is flaking?"

"Yes," she said, "but it's over five hundred years old. Isn't that to be expected?"

"Works of *this* colossal stature demand constant conservation," Armand said, annoyed. "In order to prevent them from deteriorating and vanishing right before our eyes and from history." His head spun around, only seeing two male visitors behind them walk into the chapel, as he scanned beyond them for someone to whom he could lodge a complaint. "It's appalling!" he continued to vent, as he turned his gaze back to Andrea. "I last visited this work five years ago, and since then have written countless letters to inform the diocese of the dire need to take care of this priceless piece of history. Yet, I see nothing has been done."

Armand turned his gaze back at the flaking masterpiece as his heart dropped. "Do you see how thick the varnish is?" As Andrea tried to see what he saw, he continued, "That's the result of countless restorers applying Talens Retouching Varnish over the past century."

"Isn't varnish supposed to *protect* paintings?"

Armand shook his head. "Not if it's a ketone resin varnish. It's known to delaminate paint and cause flaking." He shook his head. "Good God, this is downright sinful!"

Andrea could see the anguish that was consuming her lover and felt helpless. She was out of her element.

Meanwhile, Armand went on, explaining further about the effects of poor conservation, such as how Leonardo's masterpiece, *The Last Supper*, had flaked and deteriorated to the point of being a ghost of its former glorious self.

Off to the side, the two visitors scrutinized the masterwork, while Armand turned his analytical eyes back toward the panels. Meanwhile, Andrea looked at a few more panels, then excused herself to seek the restroom.

As the two elderly men edged their way over—one, with a face like igneous rock and in his seventies, the other, slightly younger, meticulously dressed and sporting glasses—Armand suddenly noticed them out of the corner of his eye. He turned and tried to make conversation. "Hello." He glanced at the altarpiece. "Despite its present sad condition, it's a spectacular piece of work, isn't it?"

Both men glanced at each other as the stone-faced man, with bags under his squinty eyes, looked back at Armand and replied, *"Sprechen sie Deutsch?"*

"No," Armand replied, unable to speak German, but familiar with the popular phrase. "I'm sorry."

The stone-faced man glanced at his younger, dapper friend. *"Ah, ein dummer Amerikaner, er spricht nur Englisch."*

As Armand squinted, the two men chuckled, as the older man said to his comrade, *"Wie schön es ist, kann ich in der Öffentlichkeit direkt vor diesem berühmten Altarbild sagen, dass ich die ursprünglichen Just Judges besitze."* ("How beautiful it is, I can say in public, right in front of this famous altarpiece, that *I* have the original *Just Judges*.")

As the man laughed at his own sense of daring, the dapper man nervously craned his neck to make sure the chapel was empty; to ensure that no one present understood German. As he sighed with relief, Andrea walked back in. She glanced at the two men, who furtively shifted to the other side of the chapel, while she walked up alongside Armand, who turned curiously toward her. "I can't be sure," he whispered, "but I sense those two are getting a good laugh at my expense."

"They certainly are."

His eyes narrowed. "How would *you* know?"

"I overheard him," she whispered, glancing at the two of them, then back at Armand. "I never got around to telling you; my mother was half-German. I learned to speak French and German while growing up in Bordeaux. English became my third language once we moved to America."

"Ah!" Armand replied, surprised to learn something else new about his girlfriend. Yet, his mind snapped back to the present moment. "So, what did he say?"

Andrea discreetly glanced at the older man with the stern, rocky face, then back. "Something about having the original just judges. Whatever that means."

"Are you serious?" Armand exclaimed, as his voice echoed.

Andrea grasped his arm. "Shh! They're right over there, and can surely hear us."

Armand didn't care. "Are you sure that's what he said?"

"Yes, but who are these just judges?" she whispered.

Armand motioned with his head toward the lower left panel of the altarpiece. "Those men on horseback are the *Just Judges.*"

Andrea squinted. "But they're right there, before our very eyes. Jesus, that old guy is the stupid one, not you."

"What do you mean *not me*? Did he diss me?"

She giggled while the two men shuffled quietly out of the chapel. "Well, yes. He called you a dumb American, because you can only speak English."

Armand's eyes rolled at the insult, but his mind quickly revived his pensive mood. "Well, I have news for you, he might not have been kidding."

"Oh, he wasn't kidding," Andrea explained matter-of-factly. "He seriously thinks you're a stupid American."

Armand almost had to laugh. "That's not what I meant. You see, the original *Just Judges* panel *was* stolen. It was back in 1934, and it never resurfaced."

Andrea was now even more baffled as she peered over at the panel. "Then what are we looking at? A fake? Does the diocese know that?"

Armand chuckled. "Yes, of course they know it's not the original. A copy was painted several years after the theft by a talented conservator, named Jef van der Veken, who donated the panel to make it whole again." He grasped her hand and walked her quickly out of the chapel, as his head turned toward the cathedral's exit.

The two German men were standing near the huge wooden exit doors, talking.

Armand whispered in her ear. "Whatever you do, *don't* speak German or reveal our real names."

With that, he grasped her hand and made a beeline toward the two Germans with Andrea in tow. As he made his way toward the doorway, he bumped into the stone-faced German, turned and said, "Ah, *scusami*."

The German huffed, then noticed it was the man he'd met in the chapel. He squinted. "I thought you were an American?" he said in English, with a thick German accent.

"No, I'm afraid not," Armand said, now even more curious as to why the man refused to speak English earlier. "And I thought you only spoke German?"

The man shrugged. "I prefer German." His eyes looked deeper into Armand's eyes as he tried to reevaluate the man before him. "And was that Italian *you* just spoke?"

Armand kept the faux pleasant look on his face as his curiosity about this odd, stern-faced man was mounting. "*Si*, I am Italian," he glanced at Andrea, "and my girlfriend here is French. English is only our second language."

The man's rocky face cracked into a crooked smile as he glanced at his well-dressed partner and elbowed him. "Ah, we like Italians, right Gustav?" As Gustav rolled his eyes and obligingly nodded, the older man added, "But the best thing about the French..." he peered at Andrea, "was when we occupied your country."

Andrea smirked. "Well, that didn't work out too well for you, did it?"

As the man smirked back, Gustav tried to soften his friend's crude remark, which visibly irritated him, as he replied in his thick German accent, "Please, *Fräulein*, don't mind Erik, he has a dark sense of humor." He glanced at Erik with a reproachful look. "You *were* only joking, *ja*?"

Erik said nothing.

Andrea forced herself to conjure up a fake smile as Armand interjected, "Yes, of course, I'm sure he was. How about you boys join us for a drink?"

As Andrea discreetly grasped his hand and squeezed it, the two new acquaintances glanced at each other and hesitated, while Armand ignored Andrea's silent objection and said, "The Schnapps is on me, gents. *Andiamo!*"

With that, he grasped Gustav's elbow and started to walk out the exit, with him and Andrea in tow, leaving Erik with no choice but to follow.

The foursome strolled down the street and entered *Haaz Café*. Armand formally introduced himself as Armand Santore and his girlfriend as Andrea Dejarnette, then instructed his guests to take a seat at a table, while he and Andrea ordered drinks at the bar.

As they walked through the crowd toward the bar, Andrea grabbed his hand firmly once again and hissed through her teeth, "What the hell are you doing?"

"Getting us all drinks, of course."

"You know what I mean! I have a bad feeling about those two." Nervously, she glanced back at them and smiled, then looked back at Armand. "Plainly put, I *don't* like them, especially the old crater-faced one!"

"Don't worry, sweetheart, neither do I."

"Then why are we here, buying them drinks?"

As Armand approached the bar, he pulled Erik's wallet out of his pocket and discreetly showed it to her. *"That's* why!"

Andrea's eyes bulged, while Armand thumbed through it. He gleaned Erik's full name and address, then closed it. He slipped it back into his pocket and whispered, "I swiped it when I bumped into him before, just in case they refused to have a drink with us." He ordered the drinks and said, "Oh, by the way, our trip has just been augmented—we're going to East Berlin."

Andrea almost choked, as Armand paid for the four drinks, placed them on a tray, and returned to the table with Andrea trailing apprehensively behind.

As the foursome engaged in small talk, Armand subtly lowered Erik's wallet to the floor near his chair. After Erik finished his Schnapps, he dug into his pocket for his wallet and noticed it on the floor. He simply picked it up and offered to buy the next round.

During a momentary lull in conversation, Andrea felt a need to say something. She figured, since they had met viewing a piece of fine art, she'd offer a tidbit of art news she had read about to ease relations. "So, did you hear Marc Chagall passed away recently?"

Erik looked at her through his squinty dark eyes, set deep within wrinkled bags. "Ah, yes, of course, the French *Mademoiselle* pines for the talentless Russian-French Jew. What a combo." He looked at Gustav. "What do the Americans say? Three stripes, you're out!"

Andrea smirked and was about to correct him, when Armand lightly kicked her shin, not wanting to be made out as Americans or even knowing much about them. It was essential to conceal their identities. Playing into the role, Armand replied, "Who even cares what those uncultured Americans say or do? Besides, *fútbol* is the best sport on the planet. Wouldn't you boys agree?"

"*Ja! mein* Italian *freund*," Erik said as he grabbed his glass. "Agreed! I'll drink to that."

After five more rounds, and the topic of *fútbol*—Armand's other forte and former profession—breaking the ice, Armand deftly returned to the topic of fine art. "So, Erik, as I alluded to earlier, I'm in town not only for the festival, but also to view great art... and not just the pieces in museums. You see," he lowered his voice, "I'm a fine art broker. I've made some significant purchases and sales with wealthy clients, and even prominent museums."

Erik's eyebrows rose, his curiosity piqued, as Armand rattled off a few sales he had made, all fictitious yet viable.

With the liquor loosening his tongue, Erik whispered, "That's fantastic. I happen to have in my possession two valuable acquisitions that I'm looking to sell."

Armand took a casual sip of his *Frangelico*, having switched over to the Italian liqueur in lieu of Schnapps, as he relished playing up his Italian role. "Well, I'm not sure I can handle any new transactions right now, Erik. Besides, I only deal in major works of art. I'm very selective." He took another sip, and added, "But I'm always curious to know what people are collecting, to keep a pulse on the market." He placed his glass down and leaned furtively closer. "So, what types of pieces do you have?"

As Andrea and Gustav sat mute, just observing the two—with their eyes veering back and forth, as if watching a tennis match—Erik cautiously glanced around, then back at Armand. "I'd rather not say, just yet. But, mark my words; they're both very significant works—works that I'm sure you'd love to handle. That's *if* you really broker major works of art."

Armand rattled off names of collectors, works of art, and black market transactions, many of which he knew from his own cases, as well as those of others, adding more credibility to his false resume. Yet he soon noticed that his expertise on the subject clearly went over both Erik and Gustav's heads, and it was now abundantly clear—these men weren't art professionals.

Armand was losing faith; perhaps the pieces this old, grumpy clown had in his collection were fakes. Still, he had to find out for sure. Armand had come across all sorts of thieves in his career, and not all were the sharpest tools in the shed. Some were seasoned thugs with deadly connections, while others were penny ante novices or disgruntled artists seeking revenge or justification for their unnoticed talents. Furthermore, he could see that Erik was hot to unload whatever it was he had. And that Erik had come to Belgium personally to inspect the *Ghent Altarpiece* certainly added more validity to what Andrea overheard— namely, Erik possessing the coveted *Just Judges* panel. There was no way Armand could pass this up.

Having achieved his goal, Armand agreed, but said he would meet them a day or two later, as he had business to attend to first. Moreover, he had promised Andrea he would show her the full flavor of the Ghent Festival.

In reality, the delay was to ensure that Erik or Gustav wouldn't discover they were Americans while crossing the border and going through customs into East Germany. It was imperative to travel separately.

With their rendezvous in East Berlin set, Erik and Gustav took their leave.

Andrea shook her head and looked at Armand with dagger eyes. "Jeez, I knew life would get exciting going out with a private eye, but. going behind the Iron Curtain into *Communist* Germany? Really, Armand?" Her eyes glanced back at the exit to ensure the men had left the café, and added, "And to visit two shady characters, no less?"

"Don't worry," he said. "I'll be with you all the time, or you can tour Berlin on your own while I deal with them. Besides, you have no idea how big this could be, if it pans out."

Andrea huffed. "Yes, *if* it pans out. What makes you so sure Erik has it?"

Armand reached over and tenderly grasped her hand. "Andrea, one can never be sure. That's what private investigation is all about—*investigating*. And when a lead presents itself, you have to follow it, without delay, or risk losing it. I'm sorry you happened to be with me while this all came about, but if you prefer to stay here, that's fine, I understand. I can come back to get you, once I see where this lead takes me."

Andrea peered into his alluring eyes. She knew she would follow him to the ends of the Earth, or even into the bowels of Hell, if he asked. It was just that this new feeling of being mentally and emotionally bound to another person was something she had grown far apart from, dedicating her life instead to her career after her engagement to the two-timing creep, Ron Siler, ended in disaster. She breathed heavily, as a warm and tender feeling washed away her trepidation. She leaned forward. "You're not going *anywhere* without *me*. But, I do need to know what I'm getting into with this *Just Judges* panel."

Armand smiled. "That's more like it. And you won't regret it." As the waiter served Armand a cappuccino and cheesecake and Andrea coffee and chocolate mousse, he leaned back and took a sip. "In fact, the *Ghent Altarpiece* has a fascinating history. It's been stolen, smuggled, censored, almost burned, and sold more than any other painting in history."

Andrea's eyes widened. "Well, you're off to a grand start," she said as she dug into her chocolate mousse. "Go on, you have my full attention now."

"And indeed I should, because the fact that this piece managed to survive a turbulent existence over many centuries only adds to its sublime aura. As I said, it was completed by the masterful brothers Hubert and Jan van Eyck and installed in the cathedral in 1432." Armand took another sip of his cappuccino and ate a sliver of his cheesecake, then placed his fork down. "And this is where the painting's eventful travels begin." He leaned forward. "A century later, in 1566, a group of radical Calvinists crashed through the cathedral's doors with a battering ram. Their mission: to burn what they believed was a blasphemous work of idolatry by their Catholic rivals." As Andrea's sleek eyebrows rose in astonishment, he continued, "However, the Calvinists' malicious plot failed, as the great work had been scuttled to a safe haven before their arrival."

"Dear Lord," Andrea said. "How disgraceful!"

"Agreed," Armand replied. "Dogma is extremely potent *and* volatile. As history shows, it often incites violence. Yet there was much more to come."

With that, Armand explained how two centuries later, Joseph II—the Holy Roman Emperor and enlightened ruler, who even supported Mozart's career—was offended by the nude portrayals of Adam and Eve. As such, they were censored. Copies were made that clothed the figures in bearskin cloths.

Then came the French Revolution, and the illustrious altarpiece was looted and transferred to Paris by the covetous dictator Napoleon, where it was displayed in the Louvre. However, its stay there was short lived—like Napoleon's reign—and the honorable King Louis XVIII, who ascended the throne, returned the piece to Ghent.

However, portions of it were destined to take flight once again, this time by the Ghent bishop's own vicar-general, who stole six panels and sold them on the black market. The panels eventually made their way into the hands of an art collector in Berlin, who donated them to his Prussian-German government.

At the outbreak of World War I, the German high command longed to have the entire work and attempted to loot the remaining panels. However, a valiant custodian at the cathedral thwarted their plans, having hid the panels in the bishop's residence.

Then, a ray of light shone once again. After the war, the Germans were ordered, under the Versailles Treaty, to return the six stolen panels to their sacred home in Ghent.

However, their time to bask in the sun was short lived. In 1934, two panels were stolen: *Just Judges* and *Saint John the Baptist*. Shortly after, the bishop received a ransom letter asking for one million Belgian francs. Crown prosecutor Franz de Heem was informed and entered the negotiations. Evidently, the thieves were not professionals, as they agreed to return the panel of *Saint John the Baptist* before they received the ransom money. With the precious panel back in possession, de Heem decided to make the payment; however, instead of the full one million, only $25,000 francs were inserted into the envelope. Craftily, de Heem made sure that the bills were traceable.

The thieves were enraged, and their next letter castigated the authorities, finding it "incomprehensible," and somehow making themselves out to appear as honorable and courageous men, men who risked their lives to steal precious works of art, not to mention having the decency to even return one panel before payment. However, their threats to chop up the *Just Judges* panel and send it back in pieces were not taken seriously, knowing that such an act would eliminate any further hopes of receiving the balance of the ransom money.

As Andrea sat enthralled, Armand leaned back in his chair. "And, believe it or not, that's not even the end of this long and convoluted tale."

Andrea placed her coffee mug down. "Are you serious? This painting has already lived a thousand lifetimes."

Armand managed to smile. "Yes, indeed it has." His face mellowed with thought as he poked at his half-eaten piece of cheesecake with his fork. He looked back up at her. "To be honest, it wasn't just the Ghent Festival and museums that I wanted to show you, Andrea. This mystery has gnawed at me for many years. There are so many odd occurrences that took place here, both during and after the heist."

"Well, what did you hope to…" She hesitated, perplexed. "You couldn't have known you'd bump into these German fellows at the chapel—that was purely by chance. So, what did you expect to do or find here?"

Armand sipped the last bit of his cappuccino and wiped his mouth with a napkin. "Investigate—what else? I wasn't exactly sure what I'd do first, but having bumped into these two suspicious characters, or at least Erik, I'm compelled to follow this lead wherever it goes. If, as you say, Erik claims he has the *Just Judges*, I have to go to East Berlin and see if it's authentic or a fake."

"Okay," Andrea conceded. "I'm going to put this in my head as an adventure." She paused, then added, "There's no real danger, is there?"

"Well," Armand hedged, "one never knows. They could be harmless old men who stepped into something they have no idea about, or they could be, well, they could be…"

"Could be *what*?" Andrea pressed, now concerned.

Armand waved for the waiter to bring the check, then peered back at Andrea. "Well, it has crossed my mind that, especially due to their age, they could be remnants of Hitler and Goering's art-looting squad."

Andrea's eyes widened as a slight shiver ran down her back. "You told me about your *Russian Link* case, Armand, and how you dealt with those crazy Nazi thugs. Are you saying these men might also be dangerous?"

"Andrea, I won't lie to you, there's no way of knowing for sure. But, the fact that Hitler became Reich Chancellor in 1933—one year before the *Just Judges* and *Saint John the Baptist* panels were stolen—makes it quite possible that he or Goering ordered the theft, and perhaps only managed to steal those two panels. The *Saint John* panel, as I told you, had been ransomed and recovered for $25,000 francs, but the *Just Judges* has never been found. It vanished. Oddly enough, in 1942, when Belgium had been occupied, the Nazi high command stole the entire *Ghent Altarpiece* for Hitler, minus the missing *Just Judges* panel. So, yes, Erik and Gustav could have been underlings in the Nazi Art Protection Department who stole the panel themselves or gained possession of it from the actual thieves, when chaos in the Third Reich prevailed. Countless works of art disappeared before and during the war, so it could have been hoarded, destroyed, carelessly lost, or these two men could have gotten it from Arsène Goedertier or his accomplice."

Andrea blinked, confused. "Who is Arsène Goedertier?"

"Goedertier was one of the two suspected thieves. Arsène was a wealthy stockbroker, and devout Catholic, who donated his time and money to Catholic charities. However, perhaps the greatest mystery of this missing panel occurred on the day Arsène died, when he muttered that 'he alone knew where it was.'"

"Do you suppose he lied?"

"Nothing is concrete about this case. But the fact that $10,000 francs were found in a new bank account of his, along with copies of the ransom letters, adds more silica and aggregate to the mixture."

Andrea could appreciate the analogy, with her father being a mason, but her mind was still tangled in a ball of loose threads. "So, who was the other suspected thief?"

Armand waved his hand dismissively. "I give little credence to the other suspect—his alleged involvement was only hearsay. But there are many variables in this mystery, Andrea, any one of which could lead to the truth. I think it's also worth noting that Goedertier had made another, and even more perplexing, statement on his death bed. Namely, that the *Just Judges* panel is located where neither he nor anyone else can take it without drawing the public's attention."

"How can that be?" Andrea questioned, now even more baffled.

"I don't know," Armand said. "He was either bluffing, to put us all on the wrong path, or the painting is indeed somewhere in public, yet camouflaged. It's just another unsolved—and very frustrating—riddle."

Two days later, after enjoying the Ghent Festival, Armand and Andrea rented an S-Class Mercedes-Benz and drove for eight hours. They crossed the Belgium/West Germany border and came upon Checkpoint Charlie, the only crossing point into East Berlin for non-Germans.

The armed guards at the border unnerved Andrea, while Armand opened the trunk for the inspection. One official stepped out of the booth, inspected Armand and Andrea's passports and papers, then looked back up. "Both of your personal papers are in order," he said in his thick German accent. "But where is your itinerary sheet?"

Armand chuckled. "An itinerary? Seriously?"

"Dead serious," the officer snapped, as he pushed the papers into Armand's hand and stood before him, erect and militant. "So, Mr. Arnolfini, I will ask you one last time, where is it?"

Armand calmly put the papers back into his pocket. "I'm visiting friends." He glanced at Andrea, still sitting in the car. "And I'm not sure exactly where we'll be going each day. You see, we don't live in a prison, we're *free* spirits."

The officer's ironclad face turned into hardened steel as he spat, "As a non-German, you *must* have an itinerary, Mr. Arnolfini! It should have been submitted nine weeks in advance. Do you hear me? *Nine weeks!* Not nine minutes ago!" As he rattled off the next four points he rammed his index finger into each finger on his other hand. *"Ein:* You *must* stay only at an Interhotel. *Zwei:* You *must* spend a prescribed amount of money per day. *Drei:* You *must* purchase your fuel only from designated petrol stations. *Und vier:* You *must* register with the police! You are woefully deficient, Mr. Arnolfini, not to mention how you're trying my patience! I cannot let you enter East Berlin! Turn your car around. *Mach schnell!"*

"Hold on!" Armand retorted. "I get it, you have rules, but I'm a private detective and happen to have friends in very high places, including Interpol. Get Otto Heinlein on the phone. *Mach schnell!*" he ordered with the same hard-assed inflection as the officer. "Otto will vouch for me, and might even call Willi Stoph, if you annoy him. Here's his direct number," which he barked out.

The officer's hot, steely face was sufficiently quenched, as he picked up the phone with trepidation and made the call. As he held the phone to his ear and spoke, his eyes remained glued on Armand. As Armand expected, the officer's hard, metallic face melted into a soft mellow flux as his stiff shoulders wilted. He hung up the phone and nodded begrudgingly. "*Sehr gut*, Mr. Arnolfini. You may pass." He turned toward a guard. "Open the gate, *mach schnell!*"

Armand hopped back in the car. As he drove past the officer, he waved with a clownish grin, then punched the accelerator. Glancing into the rearview mirror, Armand could see the officer clench his hands into fists and stomp the ground.

Andrea's head spun around then back toward Armand. "Must you antagonize that nasty man?"

Armand glanced at Andrea. "*You* said it, the man *is* nasty. I understand people need to get jobs in this prison, called communist Germany, but becoming a mean moron, like those running this regime, is not something any good person with morals and an ounce of self-respect would cave in to."

"I suppose you're right," Andrea replied, as she turned her gaze toward the walled-in city of East Berlin. To her, it looked like a ghost town populated with zombies. Graffiti marred broken down buildings while many pedestrians shuffled along, hunched over and with sullen faces, the oppression having a visceral impact that seeped into one's bones like toxic osmosis. "This place gives me the creeps. It even looks and feels gloomy."

"It's a sad state of affairs, all right," Armand replied. "One can still feel the ominous presence of Stalin and Hitler here."

As they ventured deeper into the city, however, they couldn't help but notice and admire the famous landmarks, such as when they approached the Brandenburg Gate.

Armand looked admiringly up at the triumphant monument, but suddenly frowned. Unfortunately, it was barricaded off and no cars could pass through the gate; having been closed once the Berlin Wall firmly shackled the city in 1961.

Armand sighed. "I hope one day they reopen this gate and let freedom reign once again."

"Some day, perhaps," Andrea uttered, not having much

faith in that proposition, especially as she looked at the forlorn faces of many of the East Germans strolling the streets.

"Ah! And there's our hotel," Armand said, as he pulled into the luxurious *Hotel Adlon Kempinski*, which was strategically located just opposite the Brandenburg Gate.

Andrea's eyes lit up. "Talk about choice location, this looks fantas—" she paused, then added, "wait! That ornery officer said non-Germans must check into Interhotels only." She looked at Armand. "How did you manage this?"

Armand smiled. "Actually, my friend—Otto Heinlein from Interpol—knows Willy Brandt, the Chancellor of West Germany. And Brandt recently started negotiations with Willi Stoph, the tyrannical Prime Minister of East Germany. So, I asked Otto to put in a favor for me with Brandt, and in turn Willi. So, here we are, without draconian regulations."

Andrea smiled. "Ah! So, wicked Willi Stoph is the PM here. That's why that border official wilted like a weed."

"A little toxic clout *does* come in handy," Armand said.

With that, the couple went inside, freshened up, and Armand phoned Erik, who invited them to his home. They ate lunch in the hotel café, and forty minutes later, they arrived at Erik's estate in the suburbs.

Armand looked at Andrea. "Impressive. Erik's mini mansion restores my faith that he might truly have the famous *Just Judges* panel after all."

Erik greeted them and welcomed the couple into the spacious foyer of his home, or rather, small castle. Built in the style of a gothic fortress, it was nicely decorated, with pointed-arch windows, several of which featured stained glass with depictions of Alexander the Great, Hannibal Barca, Julius Caesar, Attila the Hun, Frederick the Great, and what Armand perceived to be the Führer of the Third Reich, Adolf Hitler. However, the distinct mustache and features appeared to be temporarily masked.

Armand had to ask, "Is that who I think it is?"

Erik waved them into his living room. "Never mind that. Those damn Soviets intended to destroy it, but they acquiesced to my plea to merely obscure it. You see, I had a degree of pull in the Reich, and after the war, the Communists channeled me into the new regime here. I've been retired for quite some time, but my love for the Führer has never waned. Regardless of what anyone today thinks about him, Hitler was a great man. He took this country out of the toilet it had become and turned it into the most advanced nation in the world." He looked deep into Armand's eyes. "You cannot dispute how he transformed this nation, Mr. Santore. You just *can't!*"

Armand nodded. "Indeed. He indisputably transformed it, Erik. No question about it." Armand opted to omit how Hitler absolutely transformed the country, and much of Europe, into a ruinous graveyard, a wasteland that took decades and trillions of dollars to rebuild, and how he exterminated millions in the burning cauldron of a diabolical war, one forged in the fires of hubris and hatred. Armand was not here to argue politics and morals with a Nazi nutcase. He was here to hopefully rescue a great work of art from the clutches of a potential Nazi heist, or possibly an acquisition purchased or stolen from Arsène Goedertier.

"So, Erik," Armand redirected, "let's get down to business. What pieces are you looking to sell?"

Erik nodded. "I like a man who is all business. My good friend, Reinhard Heydrich, taught me much about business." He shook his head solemnly. "He died too young, though." He paused in thought as old war memories ignited a blitzkrieg of glorious visions, when Nazi Germany trampled over one nation after another, before the deathblows had begun to obliterate the Third Reich, an empire that Hitler, and every good Nazi, believed should have lasted a thousand years.

Meanwhile, Armand was growing more and more repulsed by Erik's choice of deranged friends and demonic leaders. He clearly recalled that Heydrich's *business* was in waste removal—waste in Heydrich's mind being Jews—as the sadistic bigot became the inglorious architect of the Final Solution. And despite Heydrich being assassinated by two Czech rebels, the Czech people paid dearly, as five thousand citizens were rounded up and killed in retaliation. Hitler's reprimand was swift and devastating.

Armand coughed loudly to regain Erik's attention. Startled, Erik flinched. "Oh, yes…yes, of course." He pointed to a thick wooden door with his gnarled hand. "This way…follow me."

With that, Erik led the couple down a long hallway—decorated with Nazi memorabilia, including photos of Erik standing with Himmler and Heydrich—and arrived at a large door, which opened with a rusty creak. He escorted them down into the dark and dank cellar and then led them through a labyrinth of narrow arched hallways—each lined with gothic wrought iron torches retrofitted with electric light bulbs—and came upon another thick wooden door with a padlock. Erik unlocked it, and as they entered the air-conditioned chamber, he switched on the light. Armand and Andrea halted in their tracks. There, before them, stood the *Just Judges* panel.

"What do you think?" Erik asked, proudly.

Andrea answered first. "I think it's magnificent!"

Meanwhile, Armand reserved judgment, and eventually said, "It certainly looks like the *Just Judges*, but I'll need to examine it before giving my final verdict."

Erik shrugged. "By all means. Do what you will. I'm certain it's authentic."

Armand stepped closer, and immediately, red flags sprang up. His keen eye noticed how the edges weren't sharp and meticulous, as surely Jan van Eyck's hand was. Nor was the craquelure veined or deep enough to feel appropriate for a painting well over five centuries old. He then noticed that the oak panel itself was extremely flat, without minor deviations; thus, it didn't appear to be five hundred and fifty-three years old, either.

He turned and looked at Erik. "I'm sorry, Erik. But this is a forgery."

Erik took two aggressive steps forward, coming inches away from Armand's face. "*Du Dummkopf*! I thought you were a pro?" he vented, as the varicose veins in his nose and cheeks bulged. "I'll have you know, young man, that I confiscated this panel from Arsène Goedertier. So I *know* it is authentic!"

Armand was stunned. He surmised Erik—the Nazi thief—had stolen it from Arsène—the Belgian thief—but he didn't expect the candid confession. Yet, after a quick second thought, Armand wasn't all that surprised, considering the rage flowing through Erik's Nazi veins.

"Erik," he said calmly, "I'm sorry, but I *am* a professional when it comes to works from the Renaissance to Baroque periods. And this panel is not only painted on sturdy, newer oak, but the lack of technical perfection and cracks in the paint all indicate that this is a forgery, a fake."

"You're insane!" Erik snapped. "I've had this painting in my possession for fifty-one years, ever since I took it from Goedertier. No one else ever had possession of it, other than me."

Armand turned and gazed at the painting as his mind scrambled to piece together this strange new development. If Erik did, in fact, steal this from Arsène Goedertier, then the authorities had it all wrong. Goedertier never had the original; he had *this* fake. That meant the original was somewhere else. His mind recalled Goedertier's dying words, that the painting was in public view, yet somehow camouflaged. If that happened to be the truth, then certainly this panel before him was a copy.

Armand turned back toward Erik, who was still smoldering, and said, "I know unequivocally that this is a fake, Erik, and to prove it, allow me to show you."

"What do you mean? How?" he grunted, as the bags under his dark eyes seemed to swell with contempt.

"I brought some solvents and cleaners with me. Allow me to test a small section of the painting, and I'll even pay to have it restored, *if* I'm wrong."

Erik squinted. "Why should I allow you to destroy a portion of this masterpiece, and possibly diminish its value?"

"Erik, all old paintings have gone through countless repairs by conservators, from minimal touchups to major renovations. The public isn't aware of such practices, yet that's the truth of it. And none of this will matter once I show you it's a fake."

It was clear that even the word 'fake' made Erik shudder. Yet, now with Armand's startling declaration, he just had to know for sure. "Very well," he conceded. "Do what you will. But only a very *small* section."

With that Armand fetched his solvents from the car and returned. Applying the solvent on the oil paint, Armand brushed back and forth, as layers of varnish and paint peeled away, eventually arriving at the under-painting—it was bright white.

Armand wiped away the solvent, then ran his finger over the white under-painting. He lifted his finger for Erik to see. "Do you see how chalky this substance is? It's Titanium white, which was not developed when the van Eyck brothers painted this panel in 1432. Titanium white was first used in oil paintings in 1921. Furthermore, the old masters never used white for their under-paintings. They used a burnt umber or ochre blend. They believed that by starting with a midrange value they could more easily evaluate the highlights and dark shadows of the composition. So, as I said, this is undeniably a fake."

Erik stood mute. A half-century of believing he owned a precious van Eyck turned out to be a vain spike, right in the gut. Crestfallen, Erik was numb as a doleful cloud overcame him. Yet, his melancholy evaporated when Armand asked, "You said you had another piece. May I see it?"

Erik blinked, thought a moment, then nodded mechanically with a smile. He turned and walked to the entrance of a niche, draped with a plush red velvet curtain. As Armand and Andrea approached, he unveiled the piece.

Armand recoiled. He could tell immediately that the work was in the style of Hieronymus Bosch, which even the novice, Andrea, noticed, as she blurted, "Oh dear!" Her head snapped toward Erik. "Is that a Bosch?"

Erik's smile morphed into a full-blown grin, realizing his fortunes would surely change with this fine acquisition. "Indeed it is, one that has never even been documented. A truly great find…" He looked at Armand. "Isn't it?"

Armand ignored Erik and strolled closer, his eyes scrutinizing every minute detail. The painting featured Saint Jerome, kneeling and striking his chest with a stone, while a lion lay nearby. Armand was keenly aware that Bosch admired Saint Jerome greatly, and rumor had it that he had indeed painted other versions of the saint, beyond the most famous one that Armand and Andrea had seen only a few days earlier in Ghent.

Andrea stepped beside Armand, entranced by the image. Excited, she turned toward him. "So? Is it authentic?"

Armand's eyes had already finished their analysis. He glanced at her and painfully shook his head, then spun around and looked at Erik with disappointment etched in his face. "I'm sorry, Erik. It's slightly better in execution than your copy of *Just Judges*—being that Bosch was not as technically proficient as van Eyck—but it, too, is a fake."

Erik's face started to lose its color. "This can't be!" he said, as he marched over to the painting. "Look at it again!" he demanded. "You *must* be wrong."

"Erik, Renaissance artists are my specialty. I have sold countless works and revealed numerous phonies over the years, for both prominent collectors and museums. If you'd like me to test a section of this forgery, as well, I'll gladly do so. But this is just a nice imitation. In the market *I* deal in, however, it's worthless."

"I don't believe you!" Erik snapped. "Johann Gerber happens to be an art dealer here in Berlin, and he believes it's authentic, as do I."

"Tell me, what genre of art does Johann primarily deal in?"

"What does that matter?" Erik growled, irritated. "He's a professional, in the field for forty-two years, well before *you* were even born!"

Armand looked him straight in the eye, and said calmly, "Erik, Michelangelo was only twenty-six when he sculpted *David*. Age has no bearing on one's skills. Now, you can believe you have an original here, but I know it's a fake. Just like how I know your friend Johann is not an authority on Renaissance period works. So, tell me, what does he deal in—modern art? The Impressionists? Cubists? Surrealists? Dadaists? Abstract Expressionists? *What*?"

Erik cowered with each of Armand's bulleted attacks, revealing that Armand had clearly struck a nerve or two. Erik sighed, then asked with a whimper, "Is there any way you could sell them to someone? Dupe them, for all I care, like I've been duped? I need the money."

Armand shook his head and sighed. "I'm sorry, Erik, I have no interest in trying to sell these pieces. They're cheap replicas, and in the case of the Bosch, it's not even a replica, it has no provenance." Armand was about to leave, when he stopped and looked back. "But I am curious. At this late stage of your life, why do you wish to sell them now?"

Erik glanced at the floor, his face dour, then back up at Armand. "Because I've had my fill. I've enjoyed them long enough, even though being fooled. And at this hour, it makes one think about one's heirs." He glanced at the stone walls of his mansion. "I could ill afford to maintain this estate. My savings are depleted. All I have left for my son are these two heirlooms, which I had hoped to sell and leave him millions. But now that dream is gone, just like the rich memories I had of viewing these works, believing they were painted by great masters, only to find out they're cheap frauds by unscrupulous mediocrities."

Somberly, Armand bowed his head. Then, thoughts of how the diehard Nazi and Hitler fanatic unscrupulously stole these works soon obliterated Armand's empathy. Erik was a crook and a creep. And Lord knows what Hell he had inflicted on innocent souls with his pals Himmler and Heydrich. He looked at Andrea and motioned toward the door with his head. "Let's go, there's nothing here for us."

With that, the two started to walk out of the cellar vault, when Erik said, "Hold on! Are you certain you can't sell them? With your connections, I'm sure you must know someone who would buy them. Please! I beg you."

Armand stopped and turned around. The sight was

pitiful. There was dead silence for an odd moment. Erik stood motionless and mute, lost in a melancholy mist of misfortune, as he uttered, "The truth is, I'm bankrupt. I'm hard pressed for cash. My good friend, Gustav, bailed me out for many years. But now he, too, has abandoned me. I need your help."

Armand shook his head and paused a moment, deep in thought, then replied, "I'd be doing this as a favor, Erik, because there's a very good chance I'd get stuck with them. All my clients buy the real thing, not forgeries. But, for the sake of your legacy, I'll buy one of them. Just the Bosch."

"That would be splendid. Can you manage seventeen hundred marks for it?"

Armand chuckled. "For a fake, without even a provenance—*no*, Erik. Your phony *Just Judges* at least has solid documentation for a replica. The *Saint Jerome* is pure fiction. That's why I opted for that one, because it's practically worthless, but has some charm. I'll give you eight hundred marks to get it off your hands."

Erik sighed as he glanced at the slate floor, then back up at Armand. "How about twelve hundred?"

Armand smirked. "Nine hundred or forget it. I don't need the headache."

"Very well," Erik said. "Nine hundred it is."

Armand shelled out the cash, while Erik slipped the small painting into a crate. With the transaction complete, they said their goodbyes, and Armand and Andrea loaded up the Mercedes and headed out on the autobahn.

After several minutes, Andrea looked over at Armand, who was unusually quiet. "Is anything wrong?"

Armand barely glanced at her, his eyes fixed on the road as the speedometer read 150 kilometers per hour. "Nothing. It's just that even though I duped a loathsome Nazi, there's always a tinge of remorse."

Andrea squinted. "Wait! Do you mean to say..." She craned her neck to look at the crate on the rear seat. "That's a *real* Bosch?"

Armand finally smiled and winked. "Indeed it is, and for only nine hundred marks!"

Andrea laughed. "Good God! I can't believe you. You played that so cool and aloof. I'm impressed." She paused, then squinted. "But wait, do you plan on keeping it?"

"Of course."

Andrea's grin mellowed. "Really?"

Armand glanced at her as he banked into a turn. "*Yes, really.*"

"I don't know if that's right, Armand," she said, as she craned her neck to look at the precious crate once again. "Not that I think that old Nazi shyster deserved it, but something doesn't feel right about it."

"Naturally," Armand said. "You never asked me *how long* I planned on keeping it."

"Very well," she said with a half-smile. "How long?"

"Just until we get back to Ghent. *The Museum of Fine Arts* is where this belongs, with Bosch's other version of *Saint Jerome.*"

Andrea leaned over and kissed him, as the car swerved.

Arriving in Ghent early the next day, Armand delivered the newly found masterwork to Eckerd Janssens, his friend and curator of *The Museum of Fine Arts.*

Eckerd was astonished as his eyes practically devoured the paint right off the canvas. "Armand, this is a spectacular find! Where on Earth did you get it?"

"In East Berlin. Need I say more?"

Eckerd nodded, knowing well how many pieces had found their way into Germany during both World Wars and through the black market. "Of course I trust your judgment, Armand, but as you know, I'll have to call in numerous associates to inspect it further, especially with this being a new addition to the Bosch catalogue."

Eckerd couldn't contain his exhilaration as he peered back at the work. "But judging by your keen eye *and* mine, this is a winner, all right. We have long known that Bosch had an affinity for Saint Jerome, and it's exciting to finally see another version of it." He glanced up at Armand. "So, did you have a price in mind?"

Armand grasped Andrea's hand. "Yes. One U.S. dollar. And that price is non-negotiable!"

With that, Armand turned and headed for the exit with Andrea, as Eckerd's voice boomed behind them, "I love you!"

As they exited the building Andrea hugged him. "Did you hear that? He loves you. Do I have competition?"

Armand laughed. "I hope you're not getting jealous again? After all, it's not my fault so many people love me."

Andrea chuckled. "Well, I love you the most. But, you could have asked for *something*, even a thousand dollars to pay for some of your expenses, like the purchase price, rental car, gas, and that ritzy hotel."

Armand shrugged. "What can I say? I have a soft spot, especially for certain artists. And finding a never-before-seen work by Hieronymus Bosch is reward enough. But with your penchant for numbers, perhaps I should hire you as my financial advisor."

"Perhaps you should," she said with a loving smile. "So, where to now?"

Armand maneuvered her body in the direction of the Saint Bavo Cathedral. The 292-foot tall gothic cathedral dominated the skyline, making for a picturesque view of the historic city. "Let's take a nice little walk, shall we?"

They strolled along Sint-Pietersnieuwstraat and, some twenty minutes later, arrived at the cathedral. Armand looked at the majestic façade, all the way up to the towering gothic belfry.

Andrea followed his line of sight. "It's beautiful." Her eyes lowered and focused on Armand. "So, what are we doing here, *again*?"

Armand shook his head. "I'm not sure. It's a gut feeling." He finally looked down at her. "Actually, I know *why* I'm here, but I don't know *what* I'm looking for."

"That sounds a bit perplexing."

"It sure is," he said. "You recall what I said about Arsène Goedertier's baffling riddle, right?"

"Ah, yes, of course," Andrea said. "But Armand, the painting wouldn't have been hidden out here, would it?"

Armand shrugged. "Who knows? It could be concealed behind a large plaque or behind one of those reliefs. If there was construction going on at that time, perhaps Arsène used their scaffolding to access a portion of the cathedral, which would indeed place it in plain sight, yet would be well hidden and very difficult to reach."

"Oh, dear," Andrea said as her eyes scanned the towering structure. "That means the *Just Judges* could be hidden anywhere on this huge building."

"Yes, outside *or* inside." He turned toward her. "Well, without a ladder or a scaffold, we might as well take a look inside."

As they walked into the church, they once again were overwhelmed by the massive interior and all of the possible locations where the panel could have been hidden.

Andrea sighed, disheartened. "What a daunting task."

Meanwhile, Armand headed for the Joos Vijd Chapel. She turned and followed him, and they both entered the chapel together. Once again, it was vacant, as the Ghent Festival was still in session. And while many were getting drunk on bottles of Belgian beer outside, Armand was getting drunk with admiration inside, as he once again gazed at van Eyck's masterpiece, which stood majestically before him. His eyes scanned the panels and ended on the tantalizing *Just Judges* panel; the copy made by Jef van der Veken.

Armand gazed deeply into the details of the panel, comparing it in his photographic mind to Erik's copy he had seen in East Berlin. He stood there for some twenty minutes, while Andrea stepped back, knowing better than to disturb him.

As he stood there, a streaming mixture of thoughts fermented in his head. He couldn't avoid the fact that not one, but *two* copies had been made. However, they were vastly different. Erik's copy had obvious flaws that he was immediately able to discern. Yet the panel before him seemed perfect, at least perfect in the sense of being in perfect harmony with the gifted hands of the van Eyck brothers. Armand had spent many years analyzing such works in great detail, and almost felt as if he himself had painted them, being that much in sync with the old masters.

As his eyes scanned the horses, horsemen, trees, and craggy cliffs, he felt more and more at peace and in harmony with the work. His mind suddenly rebelled with a luminous thought: *Jef van der Veken couldn't have been this exact, or this good, could he?*

He spun around. "Andrea! I need to see the bishop, at once!"

As Andrea bolted out of the chapel, he turned back to

gaze at the panel, a smile of exhilaration enlivening his once troubled face.

Moments later, Andrea returned with Bishop Léonce-Albert Van Peteghem and his entourage of six clerics.

Armand turned and look at him. "Your Holiness, I'm Armand Arnol—"

"Yes, I know who you are," the bishop interjected. "Not only from your lovely girlfriend here, but also from Eckerd Janssens, among others. Not to mention having read your many letters regarding the restoration of this work." His eyes looked at Armand intently. "Is *that* why you summoned me?"

"Well, that's something you must seriously entertain, Bishop Van Peteghem, but no," Armand said. "I wish to impart some very good news." He glanced at the *Just Judges*. "Brace yourself. Because this panel happens to be the original."

The bishop rolled his eyes. "Mr. Arnolfini, from the high praise lavished on you from Eckerd Janssens and others regarding your expertise, I would have expected a more coherent declaration. You must know that that panel is a copy by Jef van der Veken. The diocese received that many, many years ago as an honorable gift."

As the bishop's entourage nodded in agreement, and Andrea stood mute and even more baffled, Armand stepped toward the panel and pointed to various details. "It is my honest and professional opinion, Your Holiness, that this *is* the original. However, it is *also* an exact copy by Jef van der Veken."

Bishop Van Peteghem and his cadre of clerics either squinted—as if Armand were nuts—or chuckled—as if Armand were *really* nuts. The bishop twisted his lips. "I'm a busy man, Mr. Arnolfini, and you're talking gibberish. How can that panel be both, the original and a copy?"

Armand crossed his arms confidently. "Because van der Veken was *no* van Eyck. He just wasn't that good."

Again, the bishop shook his head, now exasperated. *"Please*, make some sense, Mr. Arnolfini. If van der Veken wasn't that good, what are we looking at?"

Armand turned and faced the painting. "We're looking at van der Veken's paint, Your Holiness, but he merely painted over van Eyck's work *exactly*, as if a paint by number picture, then pawned it off as his own."

The bishop's eyes rolled in thought, then stopped. He looked back at Armand. "Why would he have done such a thing?"

A cleric chimed in, "Yes, for what purpose? This makes no sense."

Armand unfolded his arms and took three steps, coming before the entourage. He looked into all of their eyes, then back at the bishop. "Because, I contend that Jef van der Veken had stolen the work from the original thief—Arsène Goedertier, who had the original and a copy, the latter now in East Berlin—and he told Arsène of his plan to paint over it and return it. That's why Arsène made his dying statement—that it was in plain sight, yet camouflaged."

A cleric interjected, "That still doesn't explain *why* van der Veken would do such a thing."

"I was getting to that," Armand said. "The minds and motivations of artists vary greatly, yet *all* artists aspire to be at least appreciated, or at most, loved, adored, and celebrated—whether for selfish reasons or genuinely altruistic ones. Jef van der Veken was a talented yet unrecognized artist. Therefore, by creating a skillful copy of one of the most admired paintings in history, Jef stood to gain a modicum of acclaim. By merely outlining and filling in van Eyck's masterpiece, Jef ensured that his name would be recorded in the history books for all time. Basically, he achieved immortality."

"That's one mighty potent story, Mr. Arnolfini," the bishop said, as he and his entourage reevaluated the once seemingly irrational investigator before them. Suddenly, they could see the light in his words.

"As I mentioned," Armand added, "Goedertier's dying words were that the work was hidden in plain sight, yet camouflaged." He turned and looked at the panel. "And here it is—it's been right under our noses for almost fifty years." He looked back at the bishop. "That's why even the reflectogram and x-ray of this panel never revealed anything awry. It couldn't detect anything suspicious, being that Jef's topical paint perfectly matched van Eyck's underneath."

Bishop Van Peteghem's face beamed with revelation. "Astonishing! Simply astonishing." He turned toward his underlings with conviction. "I want a test performed on a small section of this panel immediately! The top layer of paint must be stripped very carefully, so that we may confirm Arnolfini's startling hypothesis." As the clerics listened intently, the bishop added, "Once that's accomplished, I want a committee set up to evaluate this entire altarpiece for a complete and thorough restoration." He glanced at Armand. "Mr. Arnolfini's pleas over the past five years have been avoided for far too long. This work is indeed an epic achievement of great significance, and it must be preserved at all costs."

Armand looked at the bishop and sighed with relief. "Thank you, Bishop Van Peteghem."

Contented, Armand grasped Andrea's hand. As they were about to leave, the bishop said, "Mr. Arnolfini..." Armand and Andrea stopped and turned, as the bishop continued, "I, and the church, thank you for your efforts. Is there anything I can do to repay you?"

Armand paused only but a moment, and said, "Perhaps there is." Unexpectedly, he gazed at Andrea adoringly. "Andrea, will you be my wife?"

Andrea recoiled with shock. Instinctively, she blurted out loud, "Yes, of course!" Her voice boomed throughout the chamber, much louder than she wished, as she quickly covered her mouth, embarrassed.

As the bishop and clerics chuckled, Andrea turned red, then said playfully, "I mean, can I think about it?"

Now Armand chuckled. "Sure, as it is, you'll have to wait until I buy a ring. But, take all the time you need, sweetheart…within the span of three seconds, that is."

"In that case… Yes! Yes! Yes!" she exclaimed. As she embraced him, tears of joy flowed and laughter filled her heart as Armand clutched her like a precious work of art; in fact, more precious to him than even the *Ghent Altarpiece*, which, in Armand's eyes, was one of the pinnacles of earthly perfection.

Armand could feel his throat constricting, not realizing how emotional his impromptu declaration of love would be. Andrea was a gift of joy that fired his passions and stimulated his soul. And to be wed in this cathedral would be the icing on the cake. The devoted couple kissed and then turned toward the bishop, as Armand said, "We'd be honored if you would marry us, Your Holiness."

Bishop Van Peteghem grinned with affection. "And I would be more than honored to join both of your hands in matrimony."

With that, the bishop and clerics broke out into a round of applause, then congregated around the couple to congratulate them.

After several minutes of conversation, Armand and Andrea thanked each of them, took a last look at the miraculous altarpiece, and exited the cathedral.

As they merged into the jubilant crowd of the Ghent Festival, they couldn't help but realize a glaring fact— namely, how the masses were oblivious to what had recently transpired, for a baffling mystery had just been solved and a masterpiece would soon get a facelift to restore and preserve its landmark place in Western civilization, one that glorified both the pinnacle of human ingenuity and the sublime tenets of the celestial realm.

But as the loving couple looked passionately into each other's alluring eyes, that oddly seemed less important, as they held hands and vanished into the crowd.

Thank You

Thanks to all my readers for expressing your enjoyment with the character Armand Arnolfini. It was your show of support that inspired me to continue the series after the first two episodes, which appeared in *Short Stories II: Mysteries, Thrillers & Historical*.

Creating these additional tales was a thrilling adventure, as Armand gets involved with American greats, like P.T. Barnum and Mark Twain via their museums, while also coming in contact directly with John Lennon and Yoko Ono. The research alone is rewarding, yet utilizing that info to craft unique storylines takes great effort. The mind juggling process is exhilarating and quite mysterious, as some visions materialize almost instantaneously, while others take multiple revisions and quite a bit of finesse to tie it all together into a cohesive whole.

The Arnolfini Art Mysteries contains the complete series of short stories featuring private eye Armand Arnolfini, thus far, and are presented in chronological order. I hope these new adventures live up to the Arnolfini tradition.

Naturally, I am indebted to all the great artists who have influenced me over the years and made these fictional adventures possible. Their contributions to Western civilization are indeed to be cherished, and I feel couching them in entertaining mysteries brings their names and talents to a broader public not acquainted with their work.

To my steadfast family and friends who have supported my creative endeavors and my editors, marketers and to all the international contest judges who have voted several of my books as award winners, I am most grateful. *Thank you!*

— Rich DiSilvio

My Nazi Nemesis

GOLD AWARD WINNER

★★★★★ "DiSilvio's plot is cunning and ingenious!"
-- *Jack Magnus for Readers' Favorite*

A deadly love triangle launches a father and daughter team to hunt down a nefarious Nazi. Yet twists and turns abound, leading to a shocking climax.

Hardcover: 9780981762586
Paperback: 9780981762579
eBook: 9780981762593

A Blazing Gilded Age

INTERNATIONAL AWARD WINNER AND BEST COVER DESIGN

A riveting rags-to-riches saga about a poor family's struggle to survive amid a nation burning with ambition yet bleeding with injustice. Features, Teddy Roosevelt, JP Morgan, Mark Twain, Tesla and more.

Lauded by HISTORY/A+E and noted biographer Roger DiSilvestro.

Hardcover: 9780981762562
Paperback: 9780981762555
eBook: 9780997680720

Tales of Titans Series

Tales of Titans brings great historical figures to life with concise yet compelling essays, coupled with engaging narratives that enlighten readers to their miraculous deeds, and misdeeds, that have significantly shaped Western civilization.

This handsomely illustrated series offers readers brief biographical overviews and cogent analysis, while the quasi-fictional scenarios transport readers into a fascinating past, whereby putting flesh on the bones of several titans and offering glimpses into their hearts, minds, and actions.

Tales of Titans, Vol. I : From Rome to the Renaissance
Augustus & Livia, Vespasian & Titus, Hadrian, Constantine, Dante, Brunelleschi, Columbus, Vespucci, King Ferdinand, Pope Alexander VI & Cesare Borgia, and Leonardo da Vinci.

Tales of Titans, Vol. II: Renaissance to the Electro/Atomic Age
The Medicis, Gutenberg, Lorenzo de Medici, Savonarola, Leonardo & Machiavelli, Martin Luther, Queen Elizabeth I, Shakespeare, Galileo, Darwin, Marx, Stalin, Freud, Marconi, Edison, Tesla, Westinghouse, Einstein, Fermi and von Braun.

Tales of Titans, Vol. III: Founding Fathers, Women Warriors & WWII
Samuel Adams, Thomas Paine, George Washington, John Adams, Thomas Jefferson, James Madison, Alexander Hamilton, Ben Franklin, Sybil Ludington, James Armistead Lafayette, Elizabeth Cady Stanton, Susan B. Anthony, Harriet Tubman, Adolf Hitler, FDR & Churchill

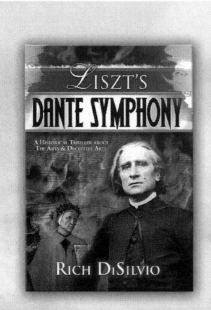

Liszt's *Dante Symphony*

A historical mystery/thriller highlighting the belligerent rise of Nazi Germany from its Prussian roots, replete with ciphers, spies, murder and a stellar cast, including Albert Einstein, Rossini, Liszt, Nazi officers and Adolf Hitler.

Hardcover: 9780981762548
Paperback: 9780981762531
eBook: 9780997680713

The Winds of Time

The Winds of Time is a historical tour de force of Western civilization by Rich DiSilvio.

With masterful style, DiSilvio paints a fascinating historical canvas with the flare of a consummate artist. Key figures and the primary cultures that literally shaped the Western world are candidly analyzed, revealing both the dark and luminous sides of mankind. Moreover, DiSilvio's insightful essays add intriguing new dimensions to the historical record.

Hardcover: 9780981762524
eBook: 9780997680706

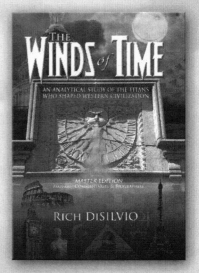

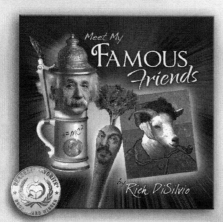

SILVER MEDAL WINNER

Meet My Famous Friends

Inspiring kids with Humor!
A whimsical picture book that pays homage to great historical figures in imaginative ways.

Author/Illustrator Rich DiSilvio presents a broad array of geniuses and heroes in a humorous and compelling fashion by altering their names and appearances, whereby making us see very familiar people in very different ways.

While children will get a kick out of looking at the comical artwork, teens and even adults will appreciate the witty play on words, inventive creations, and perhaps glean a thing or two about some of these iconic people who had a great influence on society in one form or another. Their lives and contributions have uplifted humanity in various ways, thus being great role models for young and old alike.

Hardcover: 9780997680751 Paperback: 9780997680768 eBook: 9780997680775

PURPLE DRAGONFLY WINNER

Danny and the DreamWeaver

A MS novelette by Mark Poe (aka Rich DiSilvio) about the power of dreams and the imagination.

When Danny meets Nostrildamus in his dream a bizarre journey begins!

Packed with dry humor, a mystery, and zany-looking artists, like Michelanjello & Hippopotamus Bosch, *Danny and the DreamWeaver* is an imaginative adventure of criminal intrigue and art history that demonstrates the importance of looking at life differently.

Paperback: 9780997680737
eBook: 9780997680744

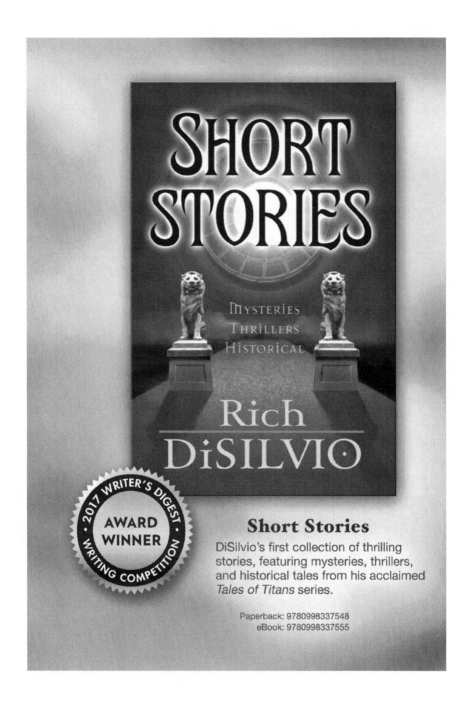

Short Stories

DiSilvio's first collection of thrilling stories, featuring mysteries, thrillers, and historical tales from his acclaimed *Tales of Titans* series.

Paperback: 9780998337548
eBook: 9780998337555

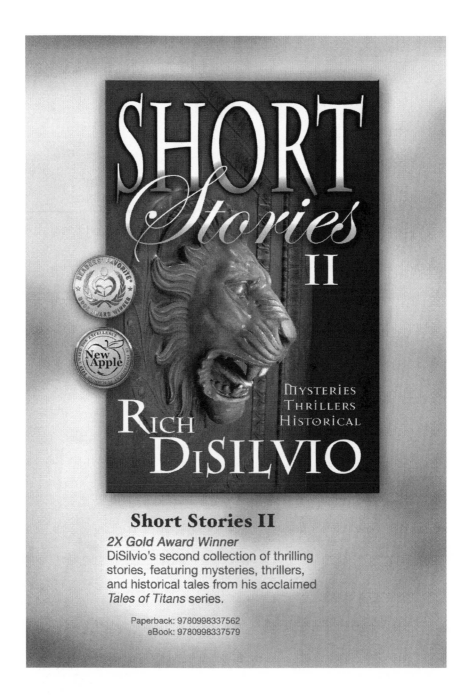

Short Stories II

2X Gold Award Winner
DiSilvio's second collection of thrilling
stories, featuring mysteries, thrillers,
and historical tales from his acclaimed
Tales of Titans series.

Paperback: 9780998337562
eBook: 9780998337579

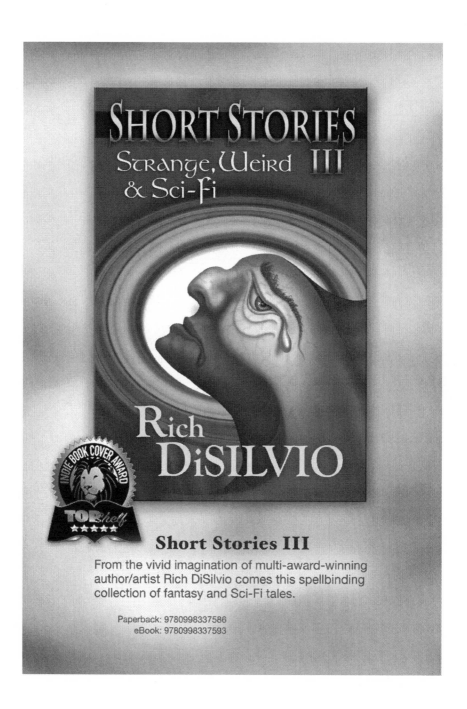

Short Stories III

From the vivid imagination of multi-award-winning author/artist Rich DiSilvio comes this spellbinding collection of fantasy and Sci-Fi tales.

Paperback: 9780998337586
eBook: 9780998337593

Short Stories IV

From the vivid imagination of multi-award-winning author/artist Rich DiSilvio comes this spellbinding second collection of fantasy and Sci-Fi tales.

Paperback: 9781950052004
eBook: 9781950052011